This Year in Jerusalem

Ben,

The great American road trip
continues. Next time in... traveling!
Hope this helps you traveling.

John F. Bako
5/29/14
- chicago

This Year in Jerusalem

Stories By Jeffrey F. Barken

Banjo Press
Baltimore
Copyright © 2013
by Jeffrey F. Barken

Contents

Acknowledgments

A word of thanks to everyone I've met on my travels. People who helped me along the way, encouraged me through their friendship and who have always kept in touch.

Special thanks to Kristin Knoerlein and Kelly Driver who helped troubleshoot, advise, and inspire the design of this book immeasurably.

For Avi

לאבי

Bells

Kurt and I were losing patience with Tel Aviv. Almost a month had passed since we'd arrived at the HaYarkon hostel and it was beginning to look like we'd been scammed. Our instructions from the consulate were to stay in the city and wait for our work visas and volunteer commissions on kibbutzim to come through. Some of the waitlisted volunteers had paid over four hundred dollars for these items, expecting work, a roof over their heads and a good experience in the country. Now everyone was running out of money and the documents weren't coming.

We were rotting. Every day we went together in a big group to the same stuffy downstairs office on Frishman Street, across from the American Embassy. There, we waited for hours only to be rejected. The room was always cramped, and some of us had to sit on the floor. To pass the time, we played chess or cards. Anyone with a computer searched for

Internet signals. Eventually, a tall woman with coiled, carrot-colored hair entered.

"Totzi'i et kulam!" she'd say. "Yesh li yeshiva achshav. No kibbutz today. You understand?"

The woman then went around the room hastily repeating her speech and making sure that all the Asians in particular understood the English. Her secretary, meanwhile, took down our names on a piece of paper. In our beginning enthusiasm, we believed it was important to arrive early and be the first on the list. Then an Israeli girl we'd met on the beach came with us to the office and wised us up about the Hebrew we didn't understand. She said the curly haired woman was saying, "Get them out of here. I have a meeting. If they sign their names to something they'll feel better."

It was morning. The sun, the ringing call to prayer from the minarets in Jaffa, the screaming mopeds, honking cars, smell of falafel and the salty sea, breezed in through the big open window of our eight-person room. The Polish kids were still snoring. I sat up straight on the top bunk, rubbing my eyes open. Then I leaned over the side and started to wake Kurt up as I'd promised him.

"Piss off," he said, swatting me away.

I tried again. This time Kurt leapt up. "Fucking hell, Myles," he yelled, trying to pull me off my bunk.

We showered, brushed our teeth and met downstairs for coffee. That was the morning routine. We had our table in the corner. The kitchen was loud and busy with everyone scrambling to get food while the breakfast spread lasted.

"Would you look at this rubbish?" Kurt complained. "Myles, I'll tell you what. I'll not take another day of this toast and fake jam. I had it better in South Africa. For Christ's sake they're charging sixty shekel each night."

Kurt had a lot weighing on this trip. There was a gang back in Johannesburg that wanted him dead. He said they'd murdered his brother when a drug deal went bad and that his mom was under police protection. His volunteer status was supposed to be the first step in the process to obtain a refugee visa. Otherwise he couldn't stay in Israel past three months.

I still wasn't sure if I believed him. He had given out this information so freely to anyone we met that the stories he told sounded rehearsed. Besides, I never saw him shed a tear for his brother or call his poor mom.

"Why would I make any of that up?" Kurt had said, one day when we were at the beach. He'd grown angry with me the moment he sensed my doubt. As proof, he showed me the massive bleeding Jesus tattoo, an emblem of gang membership that stretched across his back. Then he waded deep into the water and splashed around violently.

After that, I felt like I owed Kurt something. The week I arrived he'd shown me around Tel Aviv and helped me bargain for a better weekly rate at the hostel. But that was all in the beginning, when he was still flush with cash and optimistic about receiving a placement. Recently, he'd grown fatalistic, and he could be needy during the day. If nobody bought him food he'd neglect himself, wanting to save his money for drinks and treating girls in the evenings. I watched myself around Kurt, but when I wanted to let off steam I appreciated his friendship and was happy standing him a meal or a round at the pub. After all, Kurt was entertaining. He talked fast, was a good chess player and an excellent musician.

Now Kurt grumbled, gnawing on a crust of bread. He said feeling homesick raised an "ugly human contradiction."

"Come on. It's not that bad here," I argued.

"Eating this rot makes me want to go home already,"

Kurt said. "In South Africa at least me toast don't crumble in the toaster."

I laughed. It was hard for us to understand each other sometimes. I came from a "top country," Kurt always argued. "Nobody from the states has any perspective of poverty."

He looked pained, chewing another crust.

"Let's get out of here," I said.

"Where to?"

"Why not Jerusalem? There's a bus at ten."

He chewed, and he thought. It was obvious that he wanted to go.

"Can't. You know I haven't got the money," Kurt said, swallowing.

I wasn't surprised. For a moment, I thought of going alone, but the idea bored me. This time I wanted company.

"Whatever you don't spend with me in Jerusalem today you'll spend at the bar. Why not let's go see the country?"

"See *your* country," Kurt corrected.

I gave him a cross look and reminded him of my American passport. Then, "Suppose I spot you?" I said, pushing my plate toward him so that he could take my last piece of toast. "I know a hostel there that we can sneak into. Besides the bus, it won't cost you much."

"Please don't tempt me, Myles. I asked you not to. This is an economic decision. I can't go with you."

"Well I'm going, and, here," I said, reaching for my wallet. I drew out a crumpled blue and brown hundred-shekel note along with a few coins. The rest of my money and my passport were in a pouch under my shirt. I had kept most of it in dollars.

"That should be enough to get you through the trip," I said, sliding the money across to him. The money lay there on the table for a while before Kurt gave up protesting my generosity. He bowed his head, pressed his thumb and finger over his spiky eyebrows, and reached his big tanned hand across to grasp the bill.

"Better hurry," I said, smiling. "We'll miss our bus."

We stashed most of our bags in a hostel locker for the night. I took my guitar, and Kurt brought his harmonica. In a pinch we figured we could always try our luck playing on the street. Then we hurried to the bus station. I was glad to see Kurt's spirits brighten the more he played with that hundred-shekel note in his pocket. The whole bus ride he wouldn't stop talking about Israel.

"What a country!" Kurt said as we ascended the pine-studded hills to the capital and drove through the Forest of Martyrs. He was reading a book on the history of the Jewish State. The sight of statues and Israeli flags marking triumphs in the 1967 military campaign to reclaim the Old City made him very excited.

"They must have been mad," he commented on the men and women who had fought in Israel's bloodiest wars. "Every fight was to the finish. Tell me you're not impressed, Myles? You're going to make Aliyah and immigrate, aren't you?"

I shrugged my shoulders and was glad when we pulled into the station.

Outside it was colder than we had planned for, gray and cloudy. When I saw Kurt shiver in his shorts and tee shirt, I promised to check the hostel's lost and found for sweaters, and pointed down bustling Jaffa Street.

It was hard walking. A pair of arguing orthodox men consumed the sidewalk. Vendors pushed clothes and souvenirs in every direction, and children darted between crowds.

Kurt was relieved when I pointed out the ornate, British Mandate era building that housed the hostel, but my plan made him nervous.

"Wait here. I'll get us the code," I said, taking his bag. "There's no security after ten."

Kurt shoved his hands deep into his pockets. "Don't forget that hoody," he called after me.

Inside, I paid for a single bed in the biggest dorm, showed my passport and got the code from the little brunette who worked the desk.

"Ha malon male ha-lila?" I asked her, hoping to learn the hostel's occupancy.

"Not full yet," the girl answered, trying not to laugh at my pitiful accent.

Upstairs I snooped around until I found where they kept the extra sheets and pillows. There was a lost and found box in the kitchen. I rummaged through, finding a white pullover for Kurt and a long sleeved shirt for myself. Then I searched the cupboards for free food. There was nothing besides a box of pasta and instant coffee. In our dorm room, I slipped our bags under the bunk near the window. Then I made up the top and bottom, ruffling the sheets on both. Finally, I put everything valuable into my guitar case and left.

Kurt was glad to see me. I found him sitting on the steps across the street, shivering and playing small, slobbery tunes on his harmonica. He stopped as soon as he saw me.

"Hungry?" I asked, handing him the sweatshirt.

Kurt grinned.

I changed some dollars on Ben Yehuda Street. Then I bought two pitas and a small container of hummus for us to share. I offered Kurt a beer, but he shook his head.

"This I want to see," he said, pointing in the direction of the Old City. "I don't want to get drunk."

We started walking in that direction. The streets were winding and sculpted to the fabled hills. We walked through the little Dutch village at the edge of the New City, down the steps, past the windmill, through the gardens, along the dried out ravine and up the limestone steps to the big road and the crossing to the Jaffa Gate. The sun came out. There was that yellow glare, and we were sweating.

As we walked through the time warp into that colorful world of culture and piety, I asked Kurt if there was anything special he'd like to see.

"Everything," he said, already overwhelmed by the crowds. We found ourselves following a throng of tourists straight into the thick of things, down a sloped path that housed curtained storefronts. Tour guides were spilling English, French, Russian and German in every direction, and eye contact with the vendors was a trap.

"Ten shekel? How much you pay for this? American?" The Arabs tried everything to pull us into their stores. Jesus fish, chess pieces, rugs, beads, fabrics, dried fruit, spices, crosses, Stars of David, everything caught our eye and the vendors scoffed if we walked away.

Meanwhile there was something odd about the way people shopped. Old ladies were haggling for challa bread and hoarding food. Every transaction seemed rushed.

"Tell me it isn't Friday?" Kurt said.

I dodged his look. Neither one of us had realized we were traveling on the eve of Shabbat. Everything would shut down after sunset, and there would be no way to get back to Tel Aviv until Saturday night.

Kurt gave me a hard shove.

"Jesus Christ, I can't afford two days here. We won't eat," he insisted.

I promised him he would eat, but he still took his time calming down. Finally I convinced him to share a Nargila and some tea with me in the Arab quarter.

"My treat. I invite you," I offered repeatedly. That was the only way to keep him moving.

We entered a tunnel that lead through an Arab market. Here it was less touristy and the shops took on an air of functionality. There were children passing a soccer ball, and toy stores drawing young eyes. A barber was shearing heads inside his cubbyhole shop, and I nearly tripped over a card-board box filled with yellow, chirping chicks. The old man sitting on the stump beside his box wore a little round, blue hat, like Aladdin.

"For what you look? Via Dolorosa?" he asked me.

"Rotzim leashen Nargila. Efo efshar leashen?" I ex-plained, but he didn't understand my clumsy Hebrew. Instead, he looked me top to bottom, and, I guess, counted me a Jew. The next thing he said was, "Kotel. Wailing Wall? That way!"

I hadn't realized how close we were. Suddenly we noticed signs everywhere. "What do you say? We're right here. We'll fetch that smoke later," I suggested.

Kurt shrugged. "I want to see everything," he said again.

I led him down the path to my holy site. I don't know why it felt so familiar this time, why I fell so easily into the role of tour guide and kept waving my arms to explain things to Kurt. His eyes bulged, taking in the security, the wide open clearing packed with people and the first sight of all those skull-capped heads bobbing against the cracked limestone and green, sprig studded wall. I pointed out how the straight divide kept the men and women separate, and how the black dressed old hags distributed their red string bracelets for luck and protection against evil spirits.

"You have to write something," I said, hastily explaining the ritual of leaving a personal prayer wedged between the venerated bricks. I even fetched a pen and some paper from my guitar case.

Kurt swallowed big. I could tell he didn't like me pressuring him to be religious, yet he seemed keen to try. He asked to borrow my back so that he could write his message. Then he approached the wall.

I wasn't in the mood to pray. I was more curious what a guy like Kurt would have to say to the God of the Jews. What he might want to apologize for, pray for and question. I lingered in the background, kicking a pebble and taking in the scene. Beyond the chatter of tourists and the whispers of prayers, beyond the serious commands of the soldiers manning security, beyond the wall, coming from somewhere in that twisted up, tunneled out city, I heard bells. Sweet bells. Christian bells. They were a pleasant voice piercing the moans and wails echoing in the air.

As Kurt made his way back, I was alarmed to see him accosted by three orthodox men. They surrounded him, and I could tell he was flustered. I hurried to the rescue, barging through their swarm.

"Why you rush? Stay. You are close to God here. Don't be afraid," the men reassured us. They were harmless. They only wanted to know if Kurt, poor, hungry, homeless, Kurt, had a place to spend the Sabbath.

"You come back? Two hours. I take you to Zolty's," said the rotund man with the black and gray beard and the braided strands of Tzitzit sticking out of his black jacket. Keeping the sharp edge of his proselytizing stare on Kurt, he waited for us to give our names so that he could add us to his list of dinner guests.

Sensing our reticence, "No one should be alone on the Sabbath," his first accomplice, a younger, taller man with a stretched neck and hollow cheeks explained.

"Come. You learn something. Zolty is good man," said the third recruiter, another bearded fellow with glasses. He was even so bold as to put a wrinkled hand on Kurt's shoulder like they were old friends. "Come," he continued, rubbing his stomach. "You eat. Shabbat shalom."

We got chummy with them. Told them where we were from, how we hoped to be volunteers and explained that I was Jewish, but Kurt was not. Eventually we let them take our names down and shook hands. They were very persuasive, but we made no promises.

Outside, Kurt and I backtracked through the Arab quarter in a rush. We wanted to have our smoke before things closed. We found what we were looking for at the edge of the Christian quarter. The junction represented a neutral zone where cafes, stores juice and falafel stands were tended by men of all faiths. In the corner, some mustached men in red and white print turbans and baggy Arab dress sat at wicker tables, chomping on the metal bits attached to hoses and majestic water pipes. A cloud of thick, cold, fresh smelling smoke hovered over the scene.

Our host was so tall he had to duck to seat us in the back where there was a low beam and a big, painted-gold framed mirror hanging. He offered us tea and sugar and we asked for extra mint in our smoke.

I watched Kurt handle his harmonica, blow a few notes, then set it down on the table when the pipe arrived.

"I'm sorry those orthodox interrupted you," I said, breaking the silence.

"Don't be sorry. They're offering a free meal. Nothing wrong with that."

"You reckon you want to go?" I asked.

Kurt didn't answer. He took a long hit, and then another, let the smoke roll out of his mouth slowly, used his hands to rub the scented cloud through his hair and into his skin. He caressed his temples and behind his ears.

"Listen?" he said, pointing in the air.

"Those bells?"

"I heard them at the Kotel too. Didn't think you'd hear church bells in a Jewish city."

It was my turn to smoke. I motioned for him to keep talking.

"Bells remind me," he started to say, but then he quit. I had to coax it out of him that back home there was an English church he used to go to with his mom. He said she liked to hear the chimes.

The bells played. I passed Kurt the hose.

"This isn't right, I want to leave," Kurt said, unable to hit the pipe. The ringing tones had stirred up something inside him, and his hand was shaking.

"Relax."

"I thought this country was Jewish?" Kurt persisted. He seemed irritated that his experience should contradict whatever he had imagined about Israel.

When Kurt tried to explain, a lot of other things came out. "I suppose I'm a bit jealous," he complained. "You'll get your visa before me. You're a Jew. Of course you'll get yours. But me? I've only got three months here before the gig is up. They'll send me home. Then they'll kill me."

"That won't happen," I promised. "Tomorrow we'll go

back to Tel Aviv. We'll go straight to the volunteer office Sunday morning. I'll make a scene."

I started to reach into my pocket for more money, but that was a mistake. Before I could extract my wallet, he slapped that hundred-shekel note I had given him earlier down on the table so hard that it made our tray of tea rattle, and turned some heads.

"I can't take your money," he said. "Besides, you shouldn't get too close to me. I'm trouble."

"Really, it's nothing. I want you to enjoy yourself, take it easy."

Kurt looked me over. I guessed he was sick of having me take care of him and didn't want to be the source of my entertainment.

"Do you know how they killed my brother?" he asked. I clenched the hose, sucked a dry drag out and rearranged the charcoal in the hope of elongating the smoke.

"Happened at a night club. We was dancing with girls, you know, bloody techno music. Can't see anything in those lights. Bastard put a gun to me back. His mates drag us into the parking lot. They push me down. Put me face to the pavement, like so," Kurt said, twisting his head and lowering his face to the level of our table so that I understood the perspective. "And me brother? They pin him to the wall. Then the big fellow, the big black one, he gets down on the ground next to me, shows me his switch blade, gives me a scratch on the nose, like this!" Kurt showed me with his fingernail. "Then he whispers; 'big brother's got to pay.' You know what he does next?"

I shook my head.

"He takes that knife over to where me brother's against the wall and stabs him. Stabs him! Stabs him. Stabs him."

Kurt slapped his hands together so loud every time there was a stab that I had to raise my hand, nervous he wouldn't stop.

"Bloody church bells were ringing the whole time, " Kurt said. He looked exhausted from having related the whole thing and he bowed his head and started running that stressed hand through his hair again.

I tried the hose, but it wouldn't pull and tasted like bitter ash. Kurt waited for me to push the pipe aside before looking up again. When he did, his face had changed. His blue eyes had lost their glint. In my haste to make conversation, I tried apologizing for having dragged him to Jerusalem. Then I suggested we go to that dinner after all. "It will be good for you," I promised. "You'll be distracted."

The shofar call announcing the sunset and the start of the Sabbath only rubbed things in worse. Everyone was being called to prayer.

"Look," Kurt said, leaning back in his chair. "I can't go to dinner with you."

"Don't be embarrassed. It's Shabbat. You should experience—" I started to say, but Kurt cut me off.

"No. I want to be alone. I appreciate everything you've tried to do for me, but it won't do. Alright? You go along and get yourself dinner with Zotty? Zolty? Whatever. You go and do the Jewish thing. Leave me alone."

The tall Arab cautiously approached our table.

"Col beseder?" he asked in Hebrew, gently scooping up Kurt's hundred-shekel note and producing careful change from an embroidered purse.

I left a tip and Kurt led the way out. His mood was so heavy that I gave him his space, following at a distance. As we meandered through the emptied corridors of the ancient city, it became clear to me that Kurt was tracking the sound of those bells.

Near the Christian Quarter, he stopped, pulled the drawstrings tight on his pullover, making the white hood hug his head like he was a gnome. I watched him close his eyes, cover his lips with a hard fist and breathe through the cracks in his fingers.

"Shabbat shalom," he called back to me, waving goodbye The distance and the darkness were final proof that we were strangers. When Kurt disappeared in the shadows, I turned. Behind me the bells were counting endless hours on the steps to heaven. For Kurt's sake, I hoped they'd quit their call.

Something to Tell

The water was still warm. Ari sat on the dock wetting his toes while his mother dug through a basket of water shoes. The family dogs were barking and splashing in the lake, chasing ducks and sniffing as they swam.

Ari waded in up to his knees, letting the clapping waves wet the edges of his swimsuit. He knew this was his chance to tell his mom what had happened, but he was suddenly embarrassed. His fiancée and his childhood friend had betrayed him with their affair. That was all anyone needed to know in order to understand why he was home without Melissa and calling off the wedding. But Ari didn't think he could explain everything without letting his emotions get the best of him.

That's why he had invited his mom to take out the boat. She wouldn't judge him for losing Melissa and she would break the news gently to whoever else needed to know.

"Did you find them?" Ari asked.

Mrs. Shultz shook her head, "Your brother must have taken my pair," she said. "He's out kayaking with Dad."

"Never mind then. Come here. I'll bring the boat closer."

They were worried about the zebra mussels. That was the big discovery of the previous summer. When the Shultz family first moved into the house on the lake not even the dogs could set foot in the water without slicing a padded paw on the serrated white shells.

Ari's mom waited patiently on the dock while he rigged up the boat. She was wearing a black one-piece bathing suit and a straw hat. The yellow Sunfish rocked back and forth as small waves rolled underneath its hull. Ari tied a cleat, securing the boat to the dock. Then he ran back and forth to the bunkhouse, retrieving the rudder, mast and sail. Meanwhile, Mrs. Shultz sat down and massaged her bare feet.

Clouds were filling the sky as Ari worked. The late afternoon sun glared through the white-cotton puffs, spreading flickering light. The deep lake looked cold, surrounded by the red and orange fall foliage. The day had seemed short and Mrs. Shultz shivered when she saw the direction of the wind.

"Don't worry, we won't go too far," Ari said, making a small splash as he raised the sail and untied the cleat. The sail flapped and filled and it took some strength for him to keep the boat from running away with the wind. He waited for his mom to throw two life vests into the hold and then helped her aboard.

Mrs. Shultz smiled when she was comfortably seated near the bow and Ari had pushed them out of port. She held the sheet and Ari crawled backwards to engage the rudder. The boat wobbled with his weight until he dropped the centerboard. Distracted from their play, the dogs barked and came racing up to the edge of the dock to watch the boat depart.

Ears twitched, paws reached. Finally the lab and poodle pair yawned and lay down on the sun-warmed planks.

Taking command, Ari pumped the sail and the boat tilted gently, streaking through the water. He held the sheet down with his foot and used his back to keep the rudder steady. When a hard wind blew, he hiked out, leveling the keel. Water splashed onto his glasses. He wiped them clean with the corner of his shirt. His big hands felt dry and dirty. When he reached over the side to wet his grip, his mom curled up amidst the orange life vests. She had taken off her hat and her white streaked hair was blowing in all directions. She was already growing goose bumps from the cold spray.

"Melissa showed me the invitations," Mrs. Shultz said, watching Ari's eyes jump back and forth between the rudder and the point he had marked on the horizon. Whenever he looked her way he stared past her, eyeing the opposite side of the lake and adjusting the boat's diagonal trajectory.

"Did you pick them out together?" his mom asked. "I loved the colors."

"Melissa picked them," Ari said, then he pointed to the shoreline. "Let's come about," he said, pushing the rudder hard across the stern. The boat pivoted sharply. Ari's mom ducked the swinging boom and shifted her weight.

"I liked the other side better," she said once they were sailing on the new tack. "There was more sun."

"We'll tack again soon," Ari said. He knew he was being distant. His surprise visit home without his fiancée had alarmed everyone and his moody brooding and small talk were testing his family's patience. Bigger questions were on the tip of his mother's tongue.

"How's work?" she asked, shivering.

"The same."

Ari worked for a lobbyist in New York City. Mrs. Shultz wanted to know if he had been assigned to a particular campaign. He hadn't.

"Will you have some time off soon?"

"Don't know."

"It was a beautiful season. I wish you'd had more vacation."

"I'm sorry we didn't get up here."

"Don't feel bad. We know you're both busy. You come when you can," his mom said. She didn't ask why previous plans had fallen through.

"What's Myles going to do when you move in with Melissa?" she said, curious about his roommate.

Grunts, shrugs, mumbles: Ari was incapable of answering as he remembered the empty apartment he had come home to the previous week. As far as he knew, Myles had fled halfway around the world.

A small wake from a passing motorboat rocked their vessel and kicked some spray up over the bow. Mrs. Shultz recoiled and made a startled yelp as the water and the wind struck her skin.

Seeing his mom shiver, "We'll tack" Ari said, making good on his promise to steer the boat back into the sun. As the boat turned, Mrs. Shultz looked past Ari at their blue-painted house in the distance. She seemed to be sizing up the property.

"It's the perfect place for a spring wedding," she said.

That stung. Ari watched the water. The wind was picking up. Each wave was capped with white. He did his best to carve around their peaks and keep the boat stable.

"I guess this is the last sail of the season," Ari said.

"Can you help your dad put the boats away tomorrow?"

Ari nodded.

"We'll have to come out here once or twice this winter to get ready for the wedding," Mrs. Shultz said. "Have you thought about caterers?"

"Mom," Ari interrupted. "Can we please talk about something else?"

Everything felt raw. In the course of the weekend the numbness of his initial shock had worn off. Ari remembered barging into his apartment, ready to have it out with Myles. Instead, he found Melissa sitting on her lover's bed. She looked like she hadn't slept all night. Her short black hair was clumped and greasy. She was holding the note that Myles had left for her.

"Will you and Melissa both come out to California this winter?" Mrs. Shultz asked, calling Ari back to sailing.

"I don't know, that's Christmas time for Melissa."

"Chanukah for us. It would be nice to have her out there once before you get married."

"Right now she needs time with family."

"Is everything alright with you two?" Mrs. Shultz asked. "You have something to tell me, don't you?"

Ari's tongue felt swollen. 'What *do* you want to say?' he asked himself. He wanted a cigarette, anything to occupy his mouth in the place of speech. Shamelessly, he took out the plastic bag he'd wrapped his cigarettes and lighter in for the boat trip and lit up in front of his mom.

"What are you doing? You're smoking?" Mrs. Shultz asked, sitting upright and waving the smoke out of her face.

"Yes, Mom. I smoke now," Ari said. He seemed to expect that the cigarette would tell the story for him, but his mom looked away in impatient disgust, forced to wait out the harm he was doing to his lungs.

"If you want me to put it out, I will," he offered.

"It's not my place to tell you what to do," she said. "You're a big boy."

Ari took that to mean that he had achieved his purpose. Now she could guess. The wedding was off. He looked across the water. For a minute they were calmed in the middle of the lake. When the wind picked up again he threw away his cigarette and pulled the rudder close to his stomach, forcing a jive. The boat turned recklessly into the wind.

Now he made aggressive tacks, enjoying the distraction of competitive sporting. Otherwise, he debated going back to New York. The thought of returning to his apartment and reliving the last scene of his engagement was appalling.

"Where's Myles?" he remembered the phony, angry tone he'd used to scare Melissa when he tore his friend's letter out of her hands. The voice didn't work. She knew as well as he did that wasn't him. Ari did his bleeding on the inside.

When he read the letter, however, Melissa opened up. Mascara lines streaked down her face and Ari kept reading while she cried.

"You were pregnant?" he asked, putting the letter down halfway through. Melissa refused to look up. Ari didn't need to read the rest to know why. With him she always used protection. With Myles, there were accidents.

"It's not fair that he gets the last word," Ari said, crumpling up the letter. You should have told me."

"I kept waiting for you to come home," Melissa cried, burying her head in his hardened stomach. "You never came." She pulled him close to her and her guilty tears drenched his shirt. Ari thought of all the nights he had let her down and all the nights his work had kept him away. He knew he had been making excuses yet he wasn't ready to say goodbye to love. He wanted her back. He tried forgiving her. They hugged. They kissed. They pulled at each other's clothes. Then Ari slowed down.

"Myles went to the airport?" he asked.

Melissa nodded. "He's gone," she said. "He texted me before his plane left. He didn't say where he was going."

A wave rolled over the hull. "Ari, I'm cold." Mrs. Shultz said. She was drenched. "Can we turn back?"

"One more tack. I want to make the point." Ari said, pointing to the fork in the lake where a cliff and tall pines marked his usual sailing destination.

"That's too far. I'm soaked. I want to go home."

"The point. We're almost there."

"Ari, turn us back!" Mrs. Shultz ordered. She was turning blue. Her lips shuddered. A storm was coming in over the hills.

Ari couldn't stop. He made the tack and his mom ducked the boom.

The day was losing all its color. The sky turned gray. A fierce wind blew. Afterwards the air was frigid. Ari's mom hugged her life vest. The first drops of rain mixed with hail and pattered against the boat's hull. Ari breathed heavily and pulled the sheet in tight. He knew he was sewing up an infected wound, driving this distance between himself and his mother, the one person he'd thought he could tell.

The boat leaned to port. Ari hiked out. His mother shrieked. She was losing her grip on the edge of the hold.

Draft Dodger

Ella had never run so fast through the market. Everything blurred. She saw the bags and the breads and the colors of the clothes that were hanging. She saw the tan arms of the vendors reaching out, raking figs and dates and sculpting pyramids out of finely ground red and green spices. She heard change jingling in pockets and watched the waving hands of tourists as their tongues traded Hebrew, German, Russian, Romance: all the blended roots of Yiddish. She heard the shouting and bargaining, smelled the fried falafel and the sweet pomegranate nectar. The scene appeared like a chalked-up impressionist picture. Too much had smeared and there were no faces. Not even a solid object, it seemed, could capture her attention. She was running toward the beach.

Safe on Allenby Street, Ella straightened out her tan uniform. She found a tie in her pocket and put her straight brown hair in a knot. She was still walking very fast and was sweating. She had only one hour to meet her brother and was already fifteen minutes into her break.

"How will I even recognize him?" she worried as she crossed busy Ben Yehuda Street. She could barely remember Yoni. She knew he didn't wear glasses anymore, that he had grown his hair long and that he had lost weight. "But pictures aren't a person," she thought. "I haven't seen my brother in years."

When he called, Yoni said to meet by the pier or near the park, stuttering in search of a better landmark because he didn't remember Tel Aviv. "Come on El, meet me by that sculpture!" he said, laughing. Ella didn't share his sense of humor.

"Yoni. What are you thinking? You can't call me here," she said in English, casting nervous stares down the aisles of cubicles that filled the Central Intelligence Office where she was doing her obligatory army service. Next she was whispering in Hebrew, "Where are you? I'll come right away."

On the boardwalk, Ella strained her eyes searching for Yoni. Beyond the sand bar the wind was strong and white water waves were crashing. She wished he hadn't said the beach. She would have preferred some place less open and more private. Worried and impatient, she nearly screamed when Yoni appeared behind her and captured her in his arms. Shivering, she turned to face him. Then she didn't let go of his hug and was speaking like Babel, a mixture of English and Hebrew that was all confused thoughts.

"Nice uniform," he started to tease, stopping when he saw her face.

"Yoni, ani rotzeh, I mean I can't believe ze atah. It's you!" she said, a part of her suddenly wanting to hit him. "Mom, Dad, do they know?" she asked, crying into his shoulder.

"You shouldn't have come. I mean you can't stay here.

Can you? They'll put you in jail. Lo rotzeh. Yoni, I don't want you to get in trouble."

Yoni was laughing again. He had his dark hair up in a ponytail, two straight strands were hanging down over his eyes and he hadn't shaved.

"Don't be silly, Ella," he said, pulling her ears like he used to and holding her away from him. "Look, it's alright. I'm only stopping through. I've got friends taking care of me and it wasn't hard to get into the country. I'm here three days and then I'm gone. But you think I'd come and go and not visit my little sister?"

Ella wiped her eyes and held her brother's hand. His superior English left her envious.

"Let's walk a little? I know you don't have much time," he said, putting his arm back around her. "Which way?"

They walked south toward the Arab port of Jaffa. Seagulls were feasting on the picnic crumbs left near the playground and children were running on the grass. Yoni talked about his job in the States and how their uncle was wild. He ran a tattoo parlor in New York and Yoni had learned his business. He showed Ella the tattoo he'd gotten on his back before he left. It was a picture of Popeye the Sailor hoisting an anchor over his shoulder and flexing his sea scarred arm.

Ella gave Yoni a playful push. "Mom's going to kill you!" she said.

Yoni smiled, showing all his big white teeth. "Can't be worse than Dad and Natan," he said.

They were interrupted when a small blue ball rolled down the path, past his feet. He scrambled to catch it before it fell into the water and happily tossed it back toward the little boy who had lost his toy. "Neither of them would talk to me after I left." he said, resuming his train of thought. "Mom always tried to call."

"Aren't you worried, Yoni? Three days is too long. You should go to Jordan and get out. Anything can happen and then they'll put you in jail for dodging the draft. You'll hate it there."

Ella was the only one in the family who was sympathetic toward Yoni. They were the closest in age and had shared a room growing up on their kibbutz. Ella remembered staying up late with Yoni long after they were supposed be in bed, playing games like backgammon and gin. They'd build forts in the forest and go fishing together. When he was in high school, already dreading the army, Ella helped hide his report cards and kept his secrets about girls and planning to go abroad.

With his gifts and exciting rebellious stories, Yoni always knew how to make his sister smile. His father and his brother, Natan, on the other hand, were more serious. They had both fought in Lebanon and the hard Israeli wars left them proud, though scarred. The last time Yoni tried to contact his brother from the States, Natan called him a coward and hung up the phone.

"Look, I brought you something, a present," Yoni said, wanting to keep his sister smiling.

"Really?"

"I have presents for Mom and Dad and Natan also. Let's sit down. I'll show you. Then I'll go," he said, pointing to the big rocks overhanging the pier. "Will you give the presents to Mom and Dad?"

When they found a comfortable seat, he made Ella look inside his bag. The presents were all wrapped in used Christmas paper.

"When are you going to see them next?" Yoni asked about his parents as he handed her a little wrapped box covered with red and green ribbon.

"Yoni, what's this?"

"It's hard to find better gift wrap in New York on Christmas," he explained. Ella was impressed that he had taken the time to wrap the presents at all.

She tore off the paper and opened the small green box that was underneath. Inside, there were two pearl earrings. The pearls were held in silver leaves that dangled from the studs. Yoni watched happily as she put them on. They fit her round face perfectly.

Now Ella wanted to know about New York. She said she couldn't talk about Mom and Dad or Natan. Not now anyway. With so little time, she only wanted to hear about her brother's adventures.

"There's so much space!" he said, trying to impress her. He had been west to California. He had been south too. He had a wedding to attend in March. The wedding was in Baltimore. Then he showed Ella his American passport, full of stamps.

"You were in England, too?"

Yoni nodded. Ella handed him back his passport and reached behind her head to let down her hair, hiding the earrings he had given her. "I don't see why you couldn't have waited to go abroad," she wanted to tell her brother. She was angry with him for dodging the draft, but she didn't want to alienate him. She looked aimlessly out to the sea. The wind and spray came at her.

There was a masked splash, but the scream was unmistakable. They both leapt up to keep from getting wet and then Yoni tensed. He was the closest. The little boy with the ball had run off the edge and hit his head. Below them, the brown skinned child was unconscious, floating in the foam and slowly drifting out to sea. White-capped waves threw him against the shallow rocks.

Diana Muller.

Ella froze as her brother leapt toward the water. The boy's mother was running across the field. Everyone was yelling, but Yoni was there, he was almost there. He lay on his stomach across a rock. Another wave crashed over his head. He held on tight and in a minute they saw him drenched, spitting salt water and gasping for air. He caught the boy in his arms in the wake of the undertow. Now two other men were carefully climbing down to help. The shawl wrapped mother screamed in Arabic for her boy, her little boy! And Yoni barely managed to pass the bloodied child to the men on the rocks before another wave crashed over his head. Again he bobbed up and found his grip. He even tried to grab the blue ball that had floated near him in the tide, but he knew to reach for the hand instead. The second man grabbed hold and pulled hard. The two of them stumbled on to shore.

Sopping wet and salty, Yoni looked scared. There was no escape. He looked at his sister and he looked at the boy. He heard the ambulance and the police sirens coming. He saw two soldiers hurrying toward the rocks and he looked again at his sister.

The News From Lebanon

- August, 2006

D r. Simon Shultz knew the lifespan of a pair of glasses
as well as he knew the course of his mother's cancer.
He stood over the bathroom faucet in her Florida condo, ex-
amining his frames. They needed to be replaced but he didn't
dare leave. The ranting television, meanwhile, had driven
him from the room where the dying woman lingered.

Now Simon's head throbbed and in the dim yellow lamp-
light he hardly looked himself. His bare eyes were blue, baggy dents in his big forehead. His hairline was in noticeable
recession. Hastily, he applied a splash of alcohol-smelling af-
tershave behind his ears and along his jaw, hoping the burning sensation would jolt him awake.

Turning on a brighter light, the doctor examined his
health. He rubbed two big hands around his eyes, massaged
his tensed jaw, checked his lymph nodes at the top of his neck,
checked his pulse and stretched from side to side. Finally, he
straightened up and replaced his glasses.

Simon was anxious to hear from his wife and kids. He checked his watch. It was ten o'clock. He checked his phone. No one had called. Their flight had been delayed.

Drying his hands on a hanging towel, Simon turned off the bathroom light and peeked again into the living room. His mother lay asleep on the brown couch. The emaciated woman's eyes were strained shut and the flickering television smeared a blue haze across her pale face and swollen red ears. She was on her back, wearing a pink nightgown. Her bare, age-spotted legs fell straight across the last cushion of the sofa and her tattered gray wig was hanging on the lamp beside the couch.

Simon approached without his mother noticing. He bent over and tried listening to her labored breathing, but the blaring news program was disturbing and he turned away. He knew there was nothing more he could do to make her comfortable. The drugs she was taking had rendered her permanently numb and groggy. For her sake, he tolerated the television. She insisted on watching all the ugly news from Lebanon.

Quietly, he retreated to the kitchen. Simon wanted to believe that he was through asking himself if he would cry in the end. He had good reason to think he wouldn't. She wasn't leaving in a rush like his father had done. There'd been time to prepare for her death and he knew he'd done his best to bring some happiness into her last years. Still, his composure was tested when he opened the refrigerator.

First there came a vinegar odor. Then an empty feeling crept through him like a ghost. Two white take-out boxes contained clumps of rotting Mexican food. All the fruit had spoiled and there were several bare shelves. Where were the usual jars of pear sauce? The bread pudding? The plate of corned beef? His eyes burned at the thought of his childhood fading. In the basement he'd found boxes of pictures and home videos. Without his mother around to tell the old stories, however, could it ever be real again? He closed the refrigerator door and leaned against the appliance. The few tears that came were warm and made his freshly cleaned face feel clammy.

Simon sat down at the kitchen table. He cleared away the stacks of mail that had accumulated when his mother's health deteriorated. Then he held his hands together, as if in prayer.

He listened to the news repeat. Short clips and sound bites recorded the crackle of gunfire, sporadic explosions and sirens. There was frantic yelling as an anxious reporter interviewed civilians whose homes had been bombed. "We have to leave now," the correspondent hastily wrapped up his segment when a howling Israeli jet streaked overhead, signaling another round of reprisals. Back in New York, experts debated the likelihood of a ceasefire. Politicians critiqued history and cynically disputed Israel's war aims. Top generals were certain that Hezbollah would escalate their rocket campaign against Israel.

Simon didn't have a strong opinion. The conflict no longer absorbed his interest and he felt he had long since done his part for Israel. After all, he had married a Jewish woman under the Chuppah. Their four kids had been Hebrew schooled, Bar and Bat Mitzvahed. The family had celebrated the holidays, not with orthodox reverence, but with enough seriousness that being Jewish left a small impression on each of their lives. What more could he do?

Now, his fatigue made him question the new war's necessity, but did not diminish his pride. The harsh reality was simply a question of distance. Forty-four years old, he had to admit that Israel was very far away and that his connection to the Holocaust generation was vanishing. He'd been raised Jewish, but time and success had changed his feelings toward religion and Israel. He now felt more American than ever. His children were even less connected to the faith. They dated freely, believed that all of Israel's wars were foolish and that peace ought to be an easy recipe of humility and concessions. He thought the fast demise of the Zionist cause during his lifetime was astonishing.

At eleven-thirty his phone rumbled. His wife, Rebecca, was calling.

Simon asked Rebecca to wait while he slipped on loafers and exited the condo. His mother's place looked out on a palm shaded parking lot. In the humid night, pristine, silver Buicks and Cadillacs shimmered under yellow streetlights.

"Is she doing any better?" Rebecca asked.

"She kept her food down today. She's sleeping now."

There was a pause.

"How are you?" Rebecca asked, her voice tired and heavy.

"I'm ok. It won't be long now. Maybe another day? Where are you?"

"Airport. The boys are getting our bags. We'll take a taxi to the hotel."

"Good."

"Are you getting any sleep?" Rebecca asked.

"A little. She wakes up a lot during the night. It's hard for her to breathe and this humidity makes it worse."

"Are the air conditioners working?"

"I've got two going. I'm freezing in there. But you know how it is. The humidity is in the air anyway. It creeps in. She'll die of asphyxiation."

A hush came over Rebecca.

"Did you talk to everyone?" Simon asked.

"The kids know it's the end. Jeremy brought his guitar. They put together a little photo album for her. Is she lucid enough to look at something like that?"

"Depends. It's hard to get her away from the TV. She can't remember everything. You know her hearing is shot."

"I know. About tomorrow: What should I bring?"

"Food. I'm sorry, I've been ordering out. No time to shop."

"Anything in particular?"

"Enough for lunch and dinner."

"Alright. I will. Do you want to talk to anyone?"

"No. That's fine. I'll see everyone tomorrow. Tell the kids I say hello."

They said "good night" and "I love you." As much as Simon wanted to talk to his wife, it seemed a waste. He had no energy left to speak fluidly and all his thoughts felt jumbled. As he replaced the phone in his pocket, he noticed that he had wandered away from the condo. Now he was at the gate to the pool and he could smell the chlorine steaming in the hot tub. The cold air conditioning of the condo had clashed with the humidity outside and beads of cold sweat dribbled between his armpits and formed along his brow.

Simon entered through the gate. Inside, the place was well maintained. Lounge chairs were set up straight along the deck and the pool had been cleaned and vacuumed. The water was very still. When Simon noticed that a dried palm leaf had fallen from one of the trees looming over the wooden fence, he picked it up off the cement, pulled a chair close to the water's edge, sat down and dipped the branch in the pool. Small ripples glimmered and the water began to slosh against the gutters.

The pool was square. Simon marked its corners with his eyes. In that light, he was reminded of the King David Hotel in Jerusalem, many years ago. That was in '78, he remembered. The Yom Kippur War was still a fresh wound, but his parents were determined to take him to see their little Israel, safe and secured.

He had fond memories of the markets. They had ridden camels in the Negev, floated in the Dead Sea, walked the strip in Tel Aviv, gone north to Haifa and returned to Jerusalem for Shabbat. The sound of his mother's laughter had colored the whole trip. Back then she had a full head of curly brown hair.

His mother's loneliness after his father passed away changed her. Then she got sick. She grew stubborn as the cancer progressed, withdrawn and aloof when her hearing degenerated. Their arguments about her end-of-life care were scarring and Simon never understood his mother's decision to move to Florida.

"Why isolate yourself like that? All your friends are still in New Jersey. We're in New York. Mom, I can't get down there so easily if you have a problem," he remembered shouting into the phone. Initially he understood her desire for privacy, but not her insistence on seclusion. That was when the laughter fizzled. Despite his wishes, she did move to Florida and then for two years she would call him once a week to complain about her loneliness and ailments. He knew immediately when the cancer returned.

Her bitterness became unbearable. When they went out to eat, the service was always "too slow" and Simon cringed every time he heard his mother bark, "Waiter! This is cold, I didn't order this!" or fuss about whether or not they should tip. By now he was a regular at ATM machines, making sure he kept enough cash on hand to pay off anyone his mother insulted. When he drove her to the doctor or to the stores she liked, he was at his wit's end explaining that the gas crisis was over and that they didn't always have to search for the cheapest fill.

In this last stage of illness his mother only wanted to watch television. If he asked her for her thoughts on what she was watching, she would reply in curt, cracking mumbles. "It's the end of the world. I'm watching the end."

Her grasp of the conflict seemed concentrated on the pictures rather than on what was being said. How could she be dying like this when poor little Israel was at war? Simon had a sense that if there was anything she wanted to see worked out before she gave up on life, it was peace in Palestine. His practice had acquainted him with the search for closure that comes at the end of a person's life, but in this case he found the situation unbearable. The war in Lebanon was causing his mother to drag out a painful illness.

Despite his concerns about her suffering, Simon also appreciated his mother's resolve. Though she was born in the U.S. and was rather young at the time of the War, she grew up as though she were a survivor. Every Jew felt like a survivor when the camps were uncovered and now the Jewish State that her generation had built in response to the genocide was on the brink again. When the television flickered, showing another barrage of bombs and rockets, the same questions of identity that had haunted her entire life resurfaced. Despite her son's presence, she felt alone and far away from home.

Simon stood up. He tossed his palm branch aside and started for the gate. His thoughts had moved on to more practical matters. Getting the body to New Jersey to be buried in the family plot beside his father. Finding a suitable Rabbi to administer the funeral. Talking to the lawyers about the will. As he neared the condo he could hear someone calling.

"Rachim? He left me!" his mother was saying his father's name through the screen door. Simon hurried inside, turned on a light and was beside her as fast as he could manage.

"Oh. You're here," she said, opening her eyes and staring straight through him.

"It's me, Mom, Simon."

"I couldn't breath," she said, her voice raspy. Simon noticed how a soft tear had dribbled down her wrinkled cheek, smudging her concealing makeup. He crouched next to her, dabbed at the wet streak with a paper towel and tried to get her to sit up. She resisted.

"What time is it?" she asked.

"It's late, Mom. You should try and rest. Everyone is coming to see you tomorrow."

His mother looked annoyed.

"I said I wanted privacy" she said, raising her voice, but this only made her cough. Simon didn't say anything. They had been over this point of stubbornness and the impending reality already too many times. He waited for his mother to finish cursing as her fear and her anger and her cough, the whole spinning complex, spun toward acceptance. At last she perked up and asked, "Is Jeremy coming?"

For some reason her youngest grandson had always given her particular satisfaction in the last years of her life. Jeremy was wild and reckless, but he shared her blunt sense of humor, and she enjoyed the challenges of an unruly boy.

"Yes, of course. Everyone is coming."

"You'll have to teach him some manners, you know? Jeremy needs to put down the guitar and study."

"I'm sure he'll do fine, Mom. He's really a good—"

"And you'll want to teach him to clean up after himself. And how to make all the dishes he likes."

"Yes, we're working on it."

"He looks a lot like my son. Same measurements. 14 inches around the neck, long arms. You'll have to apologize to him for me. I didn't finish the sweater I was knitting him."

Simon let this strange comment pass. He wasn't up for trying to remind his mother who he was again.

"It will be fine, Mom. I'm sure Jeremy will love whatever you've started."

"I would have made him some pear sauce. I'm sorry. I didn't know he was coming."

Suddenly a new headline flashed across the television and interrupted their conversation. A bomb had missed its target, killing civilians. There was outrage.

"Why don't we turn this off, Mom?" Simon suggested.

"No," she protested. "I want to see how it all works out."

Disappointed, Simon rubbed his eyes under his glasses and then stood up. He asked his mother if she was comfortable. No response. He asked her if she wanted a blanket or a pillow or to move to her bedroom. No response. At last he swept his arm across the coffee table, gathering all the snotty tissues and paper towels that she had used throughout the day. Meanwhile, his mother did little to acknowledge him. She rested on her side, stared past him at the television and resumed breathing heavily.

"I'm going to get you a glass of water," Simon said, raising his voice in the hope of winning back her attention. But she was lost, watching the peace unravel.

He went and got the glass anyway. When he returned, he noticed that his mother had taken off her wedding and engagement rings and stacked them neatly on the coffee table. He showed her the glass, but she wouldn't drink.

Simon sat beside his mother and waited until she fell asleep. The opinionated reporting cycled through twice more before she shut her eyes. Finally he turned off the television and retreated into the bedroom. Initially, the silence was soothing. Later, however, the absence of voices echoing through the condo made him feel cold and he wondered if stopping the news had been the right thing to do.

As he brushed his teeth, Simon made a plan for the morning. The nurse was coming at eight. His wife would bring lunch. "What if I ask Rebecca to get some pears?" he thought. He had a vague notion that they ought to try and make one last batch of pear sauce before the end came.

Removing his bent glasses, Simon turned on the faucet. Soft, cold water washed over his hands and he splashed his face. When he turned the water off he noticed the silence again. He glanced nervously at the doorway. It didn't feel right not hearing the steady churn of news voices and the strident sounds of war coverage. The dark room beyond was also alarming. He had grown used to the television's blue flicker. Simon's heart was beating fast. He left his glasses on the counter. "I should turn the television back on," he told himself, rushing back into the living room. "Mom will want to know how it all works out."

Diaspora

"Like a puzzle, Myles! You put together," Idan said, pointing frantically at the squares and other odd shapes of grass that littered the ground. The tanned Yemenite was hastily teaching me the method for laying sod. Our boss, meanwhile, was in a hell of a mood. He paced back and forth scratching his white beard, glaring his blue, British eyes, criticizing the kibbutz volunteers for their laziness and mumbling slurs about Arabs. At intervals, a cigarette or a coffee would calm his nerves, but a phone call could send him over the edge, roaring insults in Hebrew. When a whole roll of sod was clumsily dropped from the big delivery truck, damaging the expensive turf, he stomped around screaming, "Ain't that the fucking Middle East!"

I had only been living on the kibbutz for a few weeks. I became flustered whenever we were rushed and then I could never grasp the language or the scope of a project. More patient than our boss, Idan was a good teacher and I was learning a lot from him. He figured out what Hebrew words I knew and kept an eye on me throughout the day.

That was a good thing. Without Idan, I might have gotten hurt. There was a lot going on. The trucks and the pronged grass rollers and the tall crane had appeared as though they were an army of tanks launching a surprise attack in the desert. Faster than we could snap our fingers, they rolled out stripes of green turf, streaking the yellow plane with color. Our job was to even the rows. We used pikes and hard rakes to pull the layers together and when there were gaps, we patched them with scraps.

"Like a puzzle," Idan repeated every time he caught me working slowly, but I was terribly distracted. The whole kibbutz had come out to enjoy the spectacle. Dogs marked territory. Mothers clasped hands together, thanking us and offering to make coffee. Old men and women, some of them Holocaust survivors, came out for a cigarette and these veteran settlers—the generation that had claimed the desert for Israel in their youth—proudly observed the progress of the landscape. The badlands were being made fertile. There were shouts and laughter, a mix of languages. Everyone smiled to see so many of the kibbutz children playing chaotic ball games and tag.

After lunch, it was too hot to wear a shirt. The air was so thick with dust that we gagged and sneezed. We went back to work slowly, Idan pausing at times to stretch his back and smoke his Camels. On a drink break, he admitted that he was exhausted from the project, but warned that the job would go late. Then we heard the rumbling trucks returning with another load of sod. When our boss came by, we dropped our mugs, grabbed our rakes and rushed to greet the Arab work-ers. There was another bewildering exchange of charged tongues as they maneuvered their big humming vehicles into the yard. Then the sod unfurled and we resumed our frenzied act, pulling, tugging and tying the grass quilt together.

In time, the trucks left. Our boss stood with us and sur-veyed the field. The strong sun was already drying out the move-shocked stripes of grass. "Get the hose," he ordered.

For the next hour, Idan and I ran across the yard spray-ing the grass with water until slicks of mud appeared be-tween the rows and a swift river flowed from puddle to pud-dle. When we took up the rakes again, Idan and I compared our hands. Red, bubbling blisters the size of grapes marred our palms. Our boss grinned and proudly showed off his own hard, mustard-yellow calluses. That was our cue to hurry up. Afterwards, we carried on searching for gaps in the meander-ing yard long into the afternoon, taking hell every time our boss came around to check on us.

"Come on boys, get into the fucking work!" he'd yell.

"Work slow, Myles. Now work slow," Idan whispered as soon as he was gone. The goal was to wear the man down and our tools were cigarettes, coffee breaks and a lazy reaction to the sun. I managed to work only in spurts, one minute deter-mined to finish, the next dizzy and dragging.

When I heard a fresh burst of cheerful laughter, I peered across the portion of yard that we had already finished and pressed with the tractor. The Kibbutzniks who had celebrat-ed the arrival of the grass had long since fled the sun, but a little girl—she couldn't have been more than five or six—had come outside to explore her new backyard.

I watched her find a shady spot, sit down cross-legged on the grass and then set to work unpacking a pink bag of toys.

She had Eastern features. Pale skin, a flat face and dimpled cheeks. I guessed that she was Russian or Hungarian.

Now the girl played methodically, smiling first at her small stuffed doll and next at the Tupperware cups, saucers and plastic food she had brought out for a pretend tea party. I watched her daintily serve her small guest first and then herself. Her brown curls dangled messily over her back and bothered her whenever the breeze swept strands into her eyes.

"Look," I told Idan. The girl opened a small wooden box and poured out some pieces onto the grass. "She's making a puzzle."

Idan smiled. "Let's finish," he said wanting me to get back to work, but I kept watching.

Later, we were squinting in the flickering, low sun. My back and shoulders hurt from leaning over the grass and the work seemed endless. Not even the thought of the new lawn after two months of care, when everything would have grown together lush and green, could inspire me. I didn't want to put the puzzle together anymore. I was tired and leaving the yard a mess was fine by me.

The playful girl, however, appeared in the opposite mood. She was mesmerized by her puzzling work and rarely looked up except to nudge her doll friend excitedly or to sip her pretend tea. She had pulled her hair over her shoulder, and if she couldn't immediately find a piece she stood up from her work, patiently stroking her curls until she spied the correct edge lying between the blades of grass. Perfectly silent from the beginning to the end, the finish was dramatic. She'd giggle and cackle as though bewitched. Then her face would gradually change back to innocent as she tore into her work, scattering the pieces here and there and always wider apart. A sip of tea, a hug for her doll, then she'd begin again. The challenge lay in finishing the puzzle. The fun was in breaking it apart.

The late afternoon dropped us below and beyond a curve and a crest in the new housing development's landscape. I was glad when I couldn't see the little girl anymore, somehow that laugh of hers made me feel ridiculous working so hard at a puzzle I thought was near impossible.

"What time you think we finish?" I said, simplifying my English for Idan and swiping sweat from my brow.

"Soon," he replied, pointing at our boss. "I think he needs, you know, number two?"

Sure enough, the man was acting different. His eyes were shifty and he had stiffened his stride to pinch his cheeks together. Idan and I shared a laugh. The poor man wanted to see the job completed, but his body was failing him.

"Ok, boys, over here. Quickly. That's grand. Now here. Faster, boys!" he'd yell, making us jump from job to job with the rakes. We scarcely began one project before he'd distract us with another. There were a million small, last details that needed finishing.

Finally, the boss was beat. He declined a last cup of coffee and left us standing against the backdrop of a red sky. We both sighed in relief when we heard his moped stutter and whistle happily away in the distance. Exhausted, we began collecting our scattered tools and loading the tractor.

That was when I spied what the little girl had left on the grass. Like artifacts of different moods, the girl's toys lay about the yard, frozen in the last act of her play. I remembered her mother's scratchy voice calling her in for dinner, how the girl had jumped up from her seat and left her doll sitting with the picnic plates and puzzle. She was shocked

to find green juicy grass stains across her dress and she scratched and rubbed at the discolored fabric until she realized she'd need her mother's help. Then she gave up cheerfully enough—a simple shrug of the shoulders, a little leap of joy. She dropped the corner of her dress and sprinted home, that silly, witchy laugh echoing as she flew across the lawn, leaving her toys behind.

I knelt down on the grass where she had played and thought of gathering up the puzzle pieces so that they would not be lost. The puzzle pictured cartoon zoo animals. She had assembled the pieces comprising the giraffes, zebras and elephants, but had left the corner of the gorilla's cage unfinished. I looked in a big circle and ran my fingers through the tangled grass in search of the missing pieces, but they weren't there. Meanwhile, her little doll watched over the play-scape and I had to laugh at the Raggedy Ann yarn hair, the stitched eyes like the Velveteen Rabbit and the blue button-up blouse that came down to its knees.

"Myles, what are you doing? Yallah!" Idan called. When he saw me leaning over the little girl's world of toys, it was too much. He rolled his eyes, cursed the American volunteers and started the tractor. My legs were sore and I could only walk slowly. Idan drove closer and I limped aboard the trailer. Then he sped off like a madman, launching me into the air as we ran over the curb to get onto the road.

Luckily, my joints and muscles were numb. I hardly felt the bumps on the ride back through the kibbutz. Besides, I was caught up thinking of that girl. So many times I had watched her go through the motions of Diaspora, scramble the puzzle pieces far and wide before putting them back together. I envied her acceptance of the holes and was impressed by her diligence.

As Idan backed the tractor slowly into the shed I jumped off and began unloading our cargo. Suddenly, despite my fatigue, I had a good feeling. For the first time in a long time, work was beginning to make sense. I felt eager and even a little impatient to begin again. *Tomorrow,* was all I could think as I waved goodbye to Idan and started off on my own back to the volunteer's apartment.

The Guns in Gaza

iam called me on a Thursday. He said he would be down on Saturday to pick me up. To tell the truth, his call caught me off guard. A month had passed since we'd met at the King David Hotel in Jerusalem and I was sure that he and Lilly had gone back to London.

"You're where?" Liam wanted to know. I told him about the kibbutz where I was volunteering and my work as a landscaper. "All right, that's grand," he said. "I'll look it up and be down to fetch you. I've got a car rented." At that, he hung up, leaving me with no idea what time or even where I should meet him.

When Liam called again the next day, I started to realize that this was his manner of organizing. Liam liked to build up hype.

"Gaza!" he said. "Have you any idea how close you are to Gaza?"

I laughed and said I could see the besieged Palestinian city from my window.

"Jesus. Well, I want to get as close as an Englishman can get. I want to see the guns in Gaza. Gaza, Gaza, Gaza!" he said, loving that word.

To save time and phone credit, I quickly gave him all the necessary details that our previous conversation had lacked and said a mocking, "Cheerio," before hanging up amidst his wheezy laughter.

On Saturday, I found Liam exactly where I'd said to meet. He had rented a cheap blue Fiat and parked in front of the kibbutz gate. As I approached, I found him standing in the shade of a date palm, finishing a cigarette.

We shook hands and Liam made a funny smirk. "You thought I'd be late, didn't you, Myles?" Next, he led me to the car. I threw the cooler I'd packed in the back seat and fussed with the seat belt. Meanwhile, Liam continued his speech on tardiness. "A little history lesson for you: After all, you of all people ought to know that it's the Americans who always show up late."

He was talking about the War, of course. We had only met a few times, but as far as I could tell, defensive patriotism always colored his conversations. Even now, he couldn't help boasting that, for a moment, Britain had stood alone against the Nazis.

Liam looked tense, gripping the wheel, twisting his neck, fidgeting about. I offered him his cigarettes from the cup holder in the front and then asked, "Where's Lilly?" The two of them were doing Christian peace work, teaching English in an Arab school in East Jerusalem. It was all Lilly's idea to come to Israel and I knew that the drunk in Liam disagreed sharply with the mission statement of their sponsoring organization. From his disheveled hair and stubbly chin, I gathered that they'd had a fight.

"My favorite subject," he said, rubbing his hands together and laughing. "We had a little tiff, that's all. I'm sure she'll call. Soon as she's over it."

I noticed the pillow and sleeping bag in the back. Liam's crusty toothbrush had fallen on the floor. Apparently he had been sleeping in the car.

"What's funny?" he begged to know about the smile that had suddenly crossed my face. It was absurd. I was only thinking he looked a bit like a rooster, indulging his confidence in himself like this and with his greasy hair tuffed that way.

"You are," I said, wanting him to let both subjects go easy. "You're very funny." Then I asked if Lilly was on her period.

This lit him up like a Kassam rocket. "Jesus! Yes, yes, yes!" he laughed. "I didn't think of that. Seriously, though, Myles, Lilly doesn't have to know what we do this weekend. All right? Let's go somewhere and get drunk. Come on, what do you say? Let's go down to Eilat for the weekend. Let's cross into Jordan and have an adventure. We'll find some girls. We'll get drunk."

After that, Liam smoked cigarettes and I drank beer out of the cooler. That's how we broke silences. We'd talk about beer and cigarettes. Later, Liam had some questions. "What do the people on the kibbutz say about living so close to Gaza? Jesus, it must drive them mad. Do you know anyone who has seen a rocket attack? What does everybody do? What do they say?"

I told him about the Israeli helicopters we'd seen hover over the wheat and garlic fields, conducting training missions, and the explosions we'd heard when we were out digging canals for irrigation or trimming date palms. I told him about the traumatized families we'd met whose children had gone back to wetting the bed in the wake of rocket attacks. Then I repeated exactly what I'd heard my boss and so many of my friends on the kibbutz say. "They all say Gaza is fucked."

Through the window, I could see the yellow sun and the bright blue sky. There were cotton clouds and the fields were a patched quilt of green and brown. On the right, there was the white weather balloon the Israelis had fitted with cameras and floated above the desert field that lay between the road and Gaza. Then we entered the no man's land of the undeclared war.

For a space, there was only the lonely highway stretching out in front of us. Closer in, we saw the barbed wire and green paint of a military base. Two Israeli tanks kicked up dust as they made practice maneuvers in the desert sands. Several helicopters hummed and trafficked overhead. In the guard towers, soldiers manned posts. At the end of the road, there was a walled-off, dead-end border. No passport could grant us access to Gaza without special permission and security, nor would we want to enter. American and British tourists were prime targets for kidnapping. To avoid provoking suspicion from the patrols, we quickly turned around.

"All the guns and rockets come in through the tunnels," Liam explained what he knew about the new Hamas government in Gaza. "It's a fucking mess. Nobody knows what they've got inside there now," he rambled. His jaw was clicking back and forth like a windshield wiper as he mulled so many thoughts. "A rotten jam we're in, Myles. This. Too bad a bloke always has to have an opinion these days, doesn't he? If it's on the bloody telly then you've got to have an opinion."

I didn't answer.

We found a little park off to the side of the road and decided to stop. There was a playground there and a place to grill, but we chose to sit at the edge of the lemon orchard and eat the turkey sandwiches I had packed. We could still make out the dirty, white domino high rises of Gaza City, crowding from the sea to the wall. To the south and ever widening, we saw the fault that zigzagged the fear-shadowed desert between the strip and Israel.

"It's going to be a fireworks show, isn't it?" Liam was very dire at times.

"A real fourth of July," I said, egging him on. Behind us, children pressed the buttons on informational plaques next to stone monuments. Bits of obvious Israeli propaganda, recorded in English, played on repeat. The messages explained battles fought against the Arabs and honored those who had fallen for the Jewish State.

I was sure Liam wasn't, but I thought I'd ask him anyway, "You're not Jewish, are you?"

"Nah," he shook his head. "Not me. But you are?"

I hesitated and then I explained why my feelings were complicated. In America I didn't always feel accepted as a Jew. For that reason, I had a lot of sympathy for Israel. Now that I was living in the "homeland," however, I was torn. When I looked out at Gaza I became impatient with the Israelis for not compromising with the Palestinians. On the other hand, the Palestinian rocket attacks and kidnappings were a menace. The stubbornness of both sides frustrated the West.

"I can frame the whole conflict for myself," I said, shrugging my shoulders. "But at the end of the day I'm an American here. I can't really side with anyone else."

Liam stood up and stared long and hard at the scars of war he saw along the horizon. His striped collared shirt blew and fluttered around him and he still looked tense. Tense like a boxer before a fight.

"We fucked up here, didn't we?" he said, glancing back at me. "It's as bad as Belfast." He seemed determined to play British ambassador and to make a summary of the conflict.

"What does Lilly think?" I asked, hoping for more details about their argument and an end to his rhetorical questions. Liam didn't want to talk about Lilly though. He grew silent and stared past me. After a while I mumbled some optimism.

"There's still time for a lot to happen here," I said. "Maybe some good will come?"

Liam gave me a push. Suddenly he was roaring with laughter and spouting Monty Python lines. "You Americans always know how to look on the bright side of life. Don't you, Myles?"

Walking back to the car, there was hardly anything else to say. We kicked pebbles in the dirt and both agreed that we could use a drink.

The wind blew in from the west and across the parking lot. I could feel how near we were to the sea. It even smelled a little salty there. I watched Liam drape his arms over the car door to stretch his stressed limbs and back. He tapped his fingers on the window while he waited for me to catch up with the cooler.

"She'll call," he asked about Lilly as we climbed back inside. "Won't she?"

The Smell of Garlic

First the whistle then the boom. The blast tore across the kibbutz, rattling windows and shaking the floor. We were in the shed. For a moment we all stood still and silent. Then a stack of piping fell off the shelf, kicking up dust. Explosions around Gaza were common, but never this close.

After a full day of trimming date palms with the extendable saw, we were tired. Now we woke up fast. Idan lit a cigarette and slid the heavy metal door open to look around. Outside everything was normal. There was bright sunlight. The old green tractor was unharmed. The lemon tree, the carpenter's shop, the dirt road that wound past the carrot factory, the garlic crates and the dumpster all stood in their usual place.

Nevertheless, "somebody is dead," Idan said with certainty. Twisting his greasy Yemenite beard, he sucked impatiently on his cigarette, his eyes growing red from the dry and dirty smoke. "Watch for fighters. They come now," he said, pointing at the sky.

We carried on cleaning. Bertram unloaded the trailer and I cleaned off the chain saws. The big German worked slowly for a change. He seemed distracted. Every now and then he'd peak his head out from under the roof of the shed and cautiously stare toward Gaza. When he was finished unloading, I watched him get settled in the driver's seat of the tractor. He had to push the seat back as far as it would go to make room for his long legs. Then he started the engine.

"I go to shop, Myles," he yelled over the roar as he drove away.

Idan waved him off and I walked behind the carpenter's shed to take a piss. When I came back, Idan was busy picking lemons. I uncoiled the hose and started to water the nursery plants.

"Bertram buys beer. You come over? I invite you," Idan said.

Small percussion sounds thudded like musket fire in the distance, but the trees and the hills obscured our view of the horizon. When we looked up, we caught sight of two gray Israeli fighters streaking between the clouds.

"Let's go to our place. We have a better view of Gaza," I suggested. I didn't want to go to Idan's little Kibbutznik apartment. If we did that, I knew exactly how it would end. Bertram and I would stumble home high on hash and collapse on our beds without dinner. At the volunteer's apartment things were busier and even though the two younger guys, Christian and Kenny could be a nuisance, at least we'd stay awake.

"We can make dinner?" Idan asked, trying to decide where he would be most comfortable.

"Yes. We have chicken and salad and the lemons will make a good dressing. Let's take some mint and basil too?"

Idan eyed the crop of herbs growing in a large pot beside the shed. "I can take a shower at your place?" he asked.

I nodded again. "I'll even lend you a towel."

Bertram was rounding the bend. His face was flushed with sunburn and his blond hair was filled with sawdust. He screeched to a stop in front of the shed and motioned for us to load our things.

"Any word?" I asked about the explosion.

"Something happened," Bertram said, chomping on the butt of the cigarette he had lit. "Sorry, too much Hebrew. I don't understand."

"Never mind," Idan said as we hopped on board. "We find out later."

The ride back was hard and bumpy. The green and red beer bottles that Bertram had purchased were sweating and rattling. He sped up. He slowed down. We were all obsessed with finding out where the rockets had hit. We drove past the soccer field and the shop and saw nothing. We drove past Shichun Bet and saw nothing. We drove past the dairy barns and the Thai Village. Nothing. The sun was beginning to set over Gaza. The wheat and the carrots and the garlic fields all rolled into the red illumination.

As we rounded the last bend, Idan pointed over my shoulder and yelled at Bertram to slow the tractor. Now we could see. Beyond a ridge, smoke billowed up from the garlic field in pluming balls of black and gray-filled filth. Soon, we heard the whooshing blades of an approaching helicopter, the strident yells of an ambulance and we could smell the burning garlic, dry, deep and pungent.

Bertram stalled out and had to restart the tractor. We drove around the rock wall that hemmed in the small lawn behind the volunteer's apartment and parked.

I should have known a thing like this would drive our two other housemates wild. Christian and Kenny had been itching for an eruption of violence ever since they arrived, and they raced out to greet us.

Christian, the Dane, was shirtless. He was sunburned, had his blond hair pulled back like a surfer and that silly shark tooth necklace around his neck. I still thought it hard to believe that the kid had hitchhiked across half the Arab states without being kidnapped by terrorists. Kenny, on the other hand, was drunk. His eyes went straight for the beer we had brought and he helped us unload. To him the kibbutz was only an excuse for a steady job and the Palestinian conflict was quality entertainment that got him away from his family in Ireland. He was witty, and at times I enjoyed his company. Other times he drove me mad.

"Did you see?" Christian said, pointing straight at Gaza and then at the smoking pit in the middle of the kibbutz field. "There's going to be a war!"

Nobody spoke. We all stood around and watched the smoke.

"Have you've ever seen one?" Kenny asked Bertram.

"Kassam?"

"Yes."

Bertram shook his head.

"Feck, they're a joke," Kenny said. "We find them now and again in the fields. Twisted little buggers. Wings are soldered on clumsy-like and the warheads filled with junk. They're toys compared to what the Israelis have."

On the porch, there was a chain link swing, a beat up pink couch and two plastic chairs. We all grabbed beers and settled down to watch the sunset and the big Apache helicopter descend over the smoldering crater. Kenny, meanwhile, went inside to turn on the BBC. When he found his program, he watched the "telly" like an addict and called out to us through the screen door with minute-to-minute updates.

I offered Bertram a chess match, but he declined. So did Idan. Christian sat by himself on the swing. He produced a pair of binoculars and carefully studied the damaged field.

"Medics. Look! They lift someone," he said.

We passed around the binoculars, but nobody could make out much. If somebody was hurt, they were already securely inside the helicopter.

"Who works that field?" Bertram asked.

"The Thais," Idan answered. We all got quiet.

Idan leaned back on the couch and took a deep breath of the warm garlic air. When the evening lights in Gaza flickered on he pulled out his papers and stash of hash. Then he began preparing his after-work specialty.

"We should get some more of the home-grown stuff from the Thais," I suggested when I saw what little he had left.

"Lo tov," *no good*, Idan answered. "Too dry. Burns fast. Doesn't make you high."

"But don't we support the terrorists when we buy the hash?" Bertram asked.

"A little," Idan replied. "It's smuggled from Lebanon."

I watched him scoop tobacco, burn the hash till it oozed like tar and then crumbled. He mixed everything together in a little wooden bowl, then scooped the grinds into his crinkling paper. This was not how the Thais had rolled for us. The night Pan came over to sell us pot, the tiny, smiling man had graciously offered us all he had. Eager to serve, he methodically dissected the dried green plants until there was nothing left besides a fine dust and a pile of stems. Next, Pan kneeled on the floor in his shredded work pants, placed a carefully rolled paper cone in his mouth and vacuumed the intoxicating dust off the table till the joint was suction packed.

That night, as we toked on his magic, "It good?" Pan asked constantly. He'd squint, showing exuberant pleasure every time we nodded and said, "Thank you, ka-pun kup."

Now, Idan was more deliberate. He rolled two and set them aside. He wanted to tell a story first.

"We used to go to Gaza, you know. My family."

"You could get in as a Jew?" Bertram asked.

"Yes, to go swimming, make shopping and stay at ho-tel," Idan continued. "Gaza is very popular before Intifada. I don't go now, almost eight years." When he pointed to a small white scar that made a dent in the side of his head, "You see?" he said. "Stupid kid chases me and throws rock."

We were all shocked and asked Idan a dozen questions. He made it very clear that it was an isolated, random event and that he didn't blame anyone for the violence. "Gaza is fucked, anyway," he said.

Scared of the drugs, Christian set off for a walk when he saw Idan light up. When Kenny came out to share in the joint it became difficult to get a word in. His stories were never-ending and the more he drank or smoked, the more apt he was to go on redundant tangents, criticizing America's baffling leadership and the country's excesses.

"You bought it," I said, giving my usual dismissive de-fense in the face of anti-American sentiment. I didn't have the energy to debate with him and nobody wanted to listen to us bicker in English. As the joints burned down, one by one we peeled away.

Our place was a sty. Bertram and I did our best to clean on the weekends, but it was a losing battle. The other two, who slept on cots in the hallway, were slobs. Their soiled work clothes were draped over the couch. Beer bottles stacked up on the table and dirty dishes cluttered the sink. Dirt flaked off boots, the floor needed scrubbing and the walls were smudged.

"Oh, fucking hell," Bertram said, disgusted by what he saw. Idan followed him into his room and I went to the kitchen for a glass of water. The hash hit in tremors and I was a little nauseous.

"Where's that Dane?" I called out when I saw the muddy footprints in the bathroom. I was annoyed. I had been asking Christian to mop up the apartment all week. Bertram was angry too. For days he hadn't said more than two words at a time to the kid.

Nobody answered.

I went into my square cell of a room and lay down on my skinny bed. Not long after, Kenny appeared at my door. I rolled my eyes at him and watched him sit down on the tile floor.

"Christian's gone outside again with the binoculars," Kenny said. Then he filled me in on the latest news.

"It's been confirmed," he started all over again. "Rocket attack. No known casualties yet. The Israeli's have been retaliating all afternoon."

"Stop it," Bertram interrupted. He was towering above us in the doorway and casting a dark shadow across the windowless room. Bertram had taken off his shirt. His wooden cross necklace dangled over his sunburned chest.

"What the fuck is this?" he said, holding a sopping wet towel that squished and drizzled.

Kenny shrugged and Bertram threw the thing at his face.

"You're like a kid," he yelled. "My laundry was dry. You put your wet stuff right on top. You couldn't fold my things? You couldn't make a pile?"

Bertram stormed off, ignoring Kenny's frantic apologies.

"Don't know what's got that bloke so serious," he joked afterwards. "I reckon there's a simple fix to all his troubles. We need to get properly organized. That's all. If we assign chores and keep a record this sort of thing won't happen."

I laughed, watching Kenny squirm.

"Mah?" he asked in Hebrew, one of the few words he had learned.

"Let it go," I said.

"But it's the principle, Myles. I won't have that German embarrassing me. Besides, it isn't fair. I did the dishes yesterday, but nobody noticed and now the sink's full up again. Bertram forgets. He doesn't give me any credit."

"Let it go, Kenny. It isn't worth getting worked up. Now, go get me a beer, will you?"

Kenny hardly relaxed, but he was always eager to find a drinking partner. He was gone and back again in seconds. He used his chipped tooth to open our drinks.

I could hear water running. Kenny informed me that Idan was taking that shower I had promised him and Bertram had locked himself in his room to smoke a "private joint." Christian, meanwhile, had lit a bunch of candles and was fixing a frozen pizza for dinner.

"Only ten beers left," Kenny stressed, never forgetting essential details. "We'll have to ration the rest."

The beer woke me up and then dropped me hard. Pilsner tasted like honey and each sip went straight to my head. I leaned back on my sheets and looked up at the square asbestos ceiling panels. Then I asked Kenny to hand me my guitar.

For a while, I lay there strumming mellow chords and plucking light twangy strings. Then I must have nodded off. When I came to, Kenny was still sitting on the floor playing with the bottle caps he had collected.

"Were you home already when that blast hit?" I asked, breaking the silence.

He nodded.

"Weren't you going to play football with the Thais today?"

"They canceled on us. Pan took an extra shift. Those Thais never tire. Was thirty-five degrees today, for the love of God. But you know Pan. Poor bloke's going to work himself sick."

"You don't think he was in that field, do you?"

"If he was, the Thais ought to riot. `Tis a scandal what they're put through here. Don't you think? Hazardous work environs and such rotten pay. We ought to say something on their behalf," Kenny said.

I started to laugh. The way Kenny made friends with the Thais it was like he meant to conquer them all in the end. I remembered the long night we had spent in the Thai village. I remembered their strange laughter when they asked us to choose the duck they'd slaughter for dinner, and Pan's enthusiasm when we tasted the hot chili peppers that his friends considered a test of courage.

"Me Kenny," Kenny simplified his English to the point of baby talk in order to communicate. "Kenny, friend. Ireland friend. Kenny, Ireland, good. Ireland friend. Ka-pun kup. Toda. Thank you."

"I was thinking we should have them over again soon," I said. "We need to reciprocate."

"And buy some more of Pan's smoke," Kenny added. "Now that certain folks are being stingy."

"Please don't start," I said. "You were pretty stupid with the laundry."

Kenny was about to launch into another passionate defense of his behavior when I sat up.

"Come on," I said. "Let's make dinner."

We both stumbled toward the door. When we came into the kitchen, Bertram was busy cleaning. Kenny wandered helplessly toward the television and I helped tidy up.

"One of the Thais is dead," Bertram whispered when we were standing beside each other at the sink. "It happened in the garlic field."

"Do we know who yet?"

"No," Bertram said, sighing. I reached into the fridge and opened another beer for him.

"Poor fool," Bertram said. "He probably had no idea it's dangerous here." He seemed to choke on words that split his tongue, making assumptions about the cheap labor the Israelis had imported to replace the Arabs.

"I mean what the hell," Bertram continued. "He's a fucking Thai. He only wanted work and money for his family and he didn't give a shit about Jews and Arabs, Jesus and the Holy Land. Now he's dead."

"Where did you hear about the casualty?" I asked.

"Internet. It's been confirmed."

"It was one of ours?"

"Yes." Bertram said, clearing the counter and breaking off garlick cloves to peel.

"Has anyone called the boss? He might know more," I said.

"No. But someone's been calling Idan," Bertram answered, pointing toward Idan's phone on a chair. The old Nokia was blinking wildly with messages.

"How about Kenny's boss? What's his name? We ought

to give him a call. Kenny said Pan took the night shift. There must be someone we can call."

"Pan?"

"You know Pan. The short guy with the long hair?" Kenny called over the couch. He had been eavesdropping the whole time.

"Yes," Bertram said, pausing to think for a moment. He seemed to grow increasingly uneasy with the atmosphere and his stomach let loose an unpleasant growl. I watched Bertram sniff around at that lingering smell of burnt garlic, blow his big nose violently into a tissue and put the clove he had peeled back inside the fridge. Finally, "I think we not use garlic tonight," he said, respectfully dismissing the possibility that a friend of ours was killed. "Let's make dinner?"

The cooking went slow. We were continually drawn outside to watch the fields. Our curiosity finally died out when the flames were extinguished and the helicopter flew off. We were all a little disappointed with the action. We felt sidelined as volunteers.

Idan stayed in the shower a long time. When he came out, he took his phone and announced that he couldn't stay for dinner after all. He wanted to go to his parent's house instead. Soon, Christian's pizza smelled warm and doughy in the oven, but the kid had run off somewhere and forgotten about his dinner. I took it out and offered it to Kenny.

"Tosser," Kenny snickered.

"Could you turn that off already?" Bertram asked.

Reluctantly, Kenny flicked the switch on the television and wandered outside. When it was quiet again I took a good deep breath and went to my room to grab the sheets of Hebrew vocabulary I had been learning. So long as I wasn't tired, I wanted to study while we cooked.

"Ag-vanya," I said, naming the big red tomato that Bertram was slicing when I came back. He smiled and repeated the Hebrew word. Soon the kettle boiled and Bertram prepared tea. We took turns humming Hebrew while we worked and Bertram taught me a few words in German as well. When Bertram readied the skillet with oil, I spread salt and pepper over the three chicken breasts that he had defrosted and then I rolled several of the lemons that Idan and I had picked on the table to make the juices run. As I squeezed the lemon juice out over the fry, it began to smell sweet and sour in the kitchen.

The Quiet Couple

"Something happened in India," Tomer said, hesitantly. Sarit was in the kitchen, brewing coffee.

"Nu. Don't tell," she warned.

"After the army, you need to get away from here," Tomer continued, pivoting around their secret, choosing his words carefully and explaining why they had left Israel for so long.

"Why did you come back?" I asked.

"What matters now is we are in love. That makes everything simpler," Tomer said. Then he made me repeat the word "Na-im" until I pronounced it correctly.

Naim meant pleasant and Sarit's smile as she came around with three foam-topped mugs confirmed that feeling.

We were relaxing on the couch. I was still in my work boots and they were dressed in blankets and sweats. I sensed their craving for each other in every glance and touch they shared. Tomer had grown a soft beard and his dreadlocks

made a pillow for his head. Sarit curled up beside him, kissed his cheek and adjusted her black braids.

I hadn't been in the midst of two loving partners for a very long time. They were nice to watch. So calm about showing their affections that they stirred up my loneliness and made me miss girls I knew back home.

"I want to tell Myles," Tomer said.

Sarit sipped her coffee and closed her eyes. She wasn't going to stop him.

"We are married. Nobody knows. Is too much trouble in Israel."

I was curious and I asked a lot of questions all at once.

"I don't need to go to Mikvah to prove I'm pure," Sarit argued against tradition, steadily raising her voice as she revealed unorthodox convictions.

Tomer simply refused to pay a rabbi for a right he thought was natural.

Feeling safe confiding in a foreigner, they showed me their album of wedding photos. Sarit had worn a beautiful olive green costume. Her long black hair was braided with flowers. Tomer's dreadlocks were shorter. He wore a white robe and light, baggy pants. His tan arms were decorated with colorful bracelets.

"Lots of different ways to love," Tomer said. The arrangement wasn't ideal. They wanted friends and family to know. They wanted to wear the gold rings they had exchanged on their wedding night. They even wanted to do something Jewish. But for the time being, they didn't see how they could.

"Too many people would be hurt," Sarit said, closing the book. Tomer changed the subject. He wanted to know how I liked volunteering on the kibbutz. I said it was fine, "Very "na-im?" Then I complained about the obvious things: our pay, the early mornings and the blisters on my feet.

When I asked Tomer why he drove to Jerusalem so often, he told me about the bar he managed.

"You should come by," he said. "I'm there every weekend."

"What do you do when he's away?" I asked Sarit.

"I study art."

"Show me your paintings?" I asked, pointing to the easel in the corner.

"No, I don't show yet," Sarit replied, blushing.

Her insecurity made them argue shortly in Hebrew. Tomer was pushing Sarit to be more open, but there was a lot I missed and the discussion cut off abruptly when Sarit grew frustrated.

"Di kavar!" Sarit said, jabbing him. Realizing she had made a small scene, she wanted to know how much I understood. "Are you learning?" she asked.

"Trying. Slowly."

"You'll know you've learned it when you can tell a joke," Tomer said. He offered me assistance studying and then launched into a longer discussion with Sarit in Hebrew.

In time, I understood they were talking about getting a dog. The new argument was about how big, how small, what color and if it would shed. I suggested a spaniel and Tomer scratched his head, thinking. After finishing his coffee he said he thought the dog would happen very soon.

They were also planning a big trip. Sarit wanted to go to Europe. Tomer wanted to visit the States.

"After school, after I finish. Then we go." Sarit said, growing tired of speaking English. She used it less and less and sighed whenever she couldn't find the right words.

Tomer said they would travel everywhere and then he got up to show me the garden they had built together in the back.

Outside, a little scrap-metal fence hemmed in the herbs and vines they had planted. Beyond, there was a rock wall and a pale winter sunset drifting across the green garlic into the desert. Nobody said anything and we started to go back inside.

"Will you stay for dinner?"

"No, toda, I better not. This weekend though? Yes. I'll come. Why not?"

"Tov, good. Before you go let's smoke something. Tov?" Tomer offered.

I agreed and we both fell back onto the sofa while Sarit brewed more coffee.

I asked if I could help, but there was nothing I could do. She happily cleaned my glass in the sink and boiled fresh water while Tomer carefully spread papers and mixed tobacco with hashish.

When I said goodbye, it was late. I would never have known if I had overstayed my welcome. Their home was my home, they insisted. Their laughter was genuine and even if a conversation in their other language took them somewhere very far away, it wasn't meant to displace me. They still had a lot to plan, Tomer said, explaining digressions in Hebrew. Whenever something came up that concerned their future, they preferred to settle it right away in case they'd forget. The exciting thing, Sarit said, was that now they were doing everything together.

"Lila tov, Myles. See you soon," Tomer called after me as Sarit walked me to the door.

I stepped out into the night. A silver moon was shining above the rectangular rows of houses. Somebody was burning a woodstove and the neighbors were making dinner on a grill. The scent of citrus trees and rosemary were novel comforts. Even the dark was welcome peace.

Something had happened. Maybe it was the smoke. I felt opened up. "Naim." I tried Tomer's word again, shuffling my aching feet toward the volunteer's quarters. I couldn't think of a better phrase. The simple Hebrew captured the vast dream-space of my thoughts and the contrast the new people and landscape were making against my memories of New York. The quiet kept my secret.

Digging with the German

After Idan got hurt, I always tried to talk in the mornings, but the German refused to say much. Bertram preferred privacy and a chance to smoke his cigarettes alone in the volunteer's quarters. He believed it was his fault the young man got crushed and it bothered him that the construction job was dragging. Now that the charms of volunteerism had worn off, digging irrigation trenches became the only work that set him free.

One day, he made a rule: No English before six o'clock.

"Got it?" he said as we walked to work. "I won't listen. Not 'til six."

We arrived at the shed. I checked the oil and gas in the tractor and threw the digging tools on the trailer while Bertram fixed us each a cup of coffee. The German broke his own rule when he asked, "How many sugar?" and if I had remembered the trailer-jack. I was quick to exploit his mistake, answering, "Zwei," and speaking every other nonsensical word I knew in German.

"Oh fucking hell, Myles," Bertram said. "Genug," *enough.* He pointed to the clock on the wall. We still had six minutes left of the ban on English.

I took my coffee outside and watched the sun rise over the Ruhama Badlands. Slowly the sky was filling with purple, gray and blue. Meanwhile, the dusty, Northern Negev emerged from shadow, revealing breezy wheat fields, the city of Ashkelon by the sea, unfriendly Gaza further south.

"Yallah?" the tall German said. That meant let's go.

Bertram drove and I sat in back of the trailer, legs dangling over the gray road. The old green tractor sputtered and spat smoke before the German managed to jam it into higher gear. Then we sped down the gravel driveway, past the carrot factory and up through the kibbutz. Few people were out that early.

Our boss, John, was waiting for us at the construction site. Like a punctual officer in "Her Majesty's British Army," he sat on top of his moped, sipping the morning's first cup of tea. When we approached, he tapped his watch and shook his head.

"Drive the whole way in first, did you?" John said.

Now we performed our silent ritual. Bertram passed out cigarettes and John provided his lighter. We lit up and sat down on the hill that overlooked the wreck. The ruined tractor was partially buried in dirt. Despite rains, traces of Idan's blood still speckled the bent metal frame and leather seat where a scrap of his clothing dangled.

I remembered the accident. Idan was driving the tractor. Bertram was directing him backward. The tires slipped in the mud and the tractor toppled. Idan's pant leg caught in the whirling piston and he flew ten feet.

Weak Jew? As much as we resisted, old slangs seemed to slither beneath the surface.

"Has anyone visited?" John asked.

"I have," I said. "Idan invited me to Shabbat dinner."

"Good. That's grand," John said, proud of my diplomacy.

Bertram, on the other hand, looked wary. Perhaps he was jealous. I was making the sort of peace he had hoped to establish in Israel.

"Idan looks much better," I said.

"And he is walking?"

"He walks slowly."

"His teeth?"

I said he'd seen a dentist.

"About fucking time you tried driving again," John reminded Bertram, changing the subject back to the task at hand. "I need you boys to pull your weight if we're to finish on time."

The German dashed his cigarette out and stood up. His back blocked the sun. Silence interceded.

"Yallah," John said.

We got digging.

All morning, I refused to check the time. Bertram and I took turns with the pick and the shovel. John followed, laying line and puncturing holes in the pipe for sprinklers. We dug behind the lots where I had helped Idan plant sod earlier that summer. Each yard looked a bad shade of yellow. Nobody had mowed and thistly winter weeds were growing between the grass squares.

The digging grew more tedious when we turned the corner of the first row of houses. Here along the ledge we had to even out the unfilled irrigation trenches and we had to be careful of the main pipe. This meant slow scraping with the spade and then awkward digging with the shovel. Where the ground was hard, we applied buckets of water and waited for the soil to soften. We made a big mound of loose dirt beside our trench and whenever I went to fetch a bucket of water I could see Bertram's shovel end peeking up over the pile as if he were digging a grave.

Bertram worked furiously. He smoked and he grunted and he stank of sweat. He refused my offer to take a break when John boiled a kettle.

"Take it easy," John said, but Bertram kept swinging his shovel.

I sat down with John on the hill, sipped warm coffee and waited for Bertram to quit and bring around his Marlboros.

"There's my German work horse," John joked, watching the giant dig out our trenches. "How efficient."

"He blames himself," I said, sensing my chance to confide.

"No. He blames his father."

"A Nazi?" I asked.

"Who knows what. Something about family scares him."

"Come on, John. He feels guilty about Idan, that's all. He's sincere."

"Of course he's sincere," John said, grinning as he imagined a joke at my expense. "He's the only bloody worker out there."

"He's got integrity. I respect that," I said, backing off. I didn't want John calling me lazy.

"But you're a bleeding member of the tribe. Your comrade over there probably feels left alone with an impossible lot to prove."

"He doesn't have to prove anything. Bertram is a fool if he thinks it's his fault what happened," I said.

John agreed. "The kid shouldn't have been driving in the first place. If anything, it's my fault."

I scooped more instant coffee into each of our cups, drained the kettle and brought out the biscuits and jam. John, meanwhile, kept lecturing.

"Let's hope all he's mad about is the mess he's made of the tractor. Germans can't stand it when they've made a mess."

I was supposed to laugh, but I didn't. John spread jam over his biscuit and waited for me to carry on reporting.

"Either way he's not himself," I told the rest of what I had observed back at the volunteer's apartment. "Bertram doesn't talk to anyone. He says he's born again Christian now. He's been praying to Jesus every night, wears that cross and he's quit drinking."

"You'd want to cleanse yourself too. Wouldn't you, Myles?"

"At my own pace, anyhow," I answered.

"If he's that torn up about the accident he ought to leave. Don't you think? Go back to Germany. Get some peace on his own terms."

"Maybe it's worse back home. Who knows, John? I wouldn't ask him."

Our break was over. John stood up.

"Help me look after him, will you? I can't have old Bertram quit now when were behind schedule."

John went home for lunch. Bertram and I kept digging. The hungrier we got, the more we talked. Speaking about Idan's lazy antics made us nostalgic. Before the accident, work had been fun. The Yemenite Kibbutznik knew better than anyone how to dodge a job. He had a keen nose for the

ripe fruit that we could pick and an ear for John's approaching moped. During breaks, he always illuminated Israel's history with whimsical lectures and cynical humor. He had nicknamed our boss, "John of the Negev."

When little jokes got us comparing work ethics in different countries, we found ourselves competing to find a buried pipe. Out spewed all the pent-up pride. We threw dirt behind us like steam shovels. I called Bertram a Kraut and he called me an Ami. In some ways it was fun to stereotype, but as much as we laughed in the midst of our work, each burst of lip pinched nerves we'd hoped were numb.

Bertram was ashamed afterwards. We sat on the hill and split his last cigarette.

"I don't mean it," he said. "I'm sorry about this morning too. I don't want to shut you up. I'm sick of translating all my thoughts. That's all."

"John's worried about you," I admitted.

"John's too fast to judge. He puts me on the defensive."

"He wants you to stay. Don't be paranoid," I said. "Nobody on the kibbutz is angry at you."

"Except Idan."

"You're wrong. Idan isn't mad at all. He even said he wants to see you. Don't forget you saved his life when you pulled him out. You have to try and laugh a little."

I did my best to reassure Bertram, but he was depressed and digging in deep. He reached under the collar of his shirt and brought up that cross through which he'd been praying. Suddenly he yanked the wooden charm off its string. When he threw it away, I knew he didn't have the words to say what he meant to God or to anyone.

Someone was coming down the path. The little round man in the distance waved to us. As he got closer, I saw he was older. He came slowly across the yard, chewing on a piece of baguette.

"Shalom," the man beamed, carefully fitting the loaf into his shirt pocket. I stared up at his odd figure. He was short, had not a hair left on his head, but a gray hairy chest protruding from his unbuttoned Hawaiian tee shirt. His brown eyes were hidden behind thick, square glasses.

"Ernst," he said, introducing himself. Smiling, he proudly held his round belly as though he were pregnant. Then he looked me in the eye and changed his accent, "Ich höre, sie sind deutsche?"

I didn't understand a word of his German and hastily pointed to Bertram. Gradually, I learned that Ernst had heard from his neighbor that there was a German among the volunteers. He wanted to greet him.

Now Ernst was overjoyed to meet someone with whom he could converse in the old country's tongue. The two leapt into dialogue, trying to discover where in Germany they were each from, where had the other attended school, anything they might hold in common despite the years between them.

Voices rose. For the first time in a month I heard Bertram laugh. Finally, the two shook hands again and began stepping around the holes we had dug, making their way toward the path.

"Come, Myles," Bertram directed me to follow. "He invites us."

Ernst wanted to show us his home. This was the first time we had ever ventured inside one of the new houses we had helped build. Each house on the block was identical. Four white walls and a red-shingled roof. The old man led us down the path, still speaking jubilant German and cradling his big belly.

"Mittagessen," he said, putting a hand to his mouth. This I understood. He wanted to share his lunch.

Ernst's place stank of neglect, rotting food and moth-balls. Caked dirt crumbled off our boots across the tile floor.

"Won't John mind us taking such a long break?" I asked Bertram as we passed into the cluttered living room.

Ernst overheard. "You not worry about John," he said. "Englishman's garden can wait."

As eager as they both were to speak German, Ernst and Bertram did me a great honor once we were in the kitchen, continuing in English.

"Coffee? Tea. You drink Schnapps?" the little man said, scurrying around and procuring glasses.

Bertram declined the alcohol, but I enjoyed a taste. Next thing we knew, Ernst was unveiling all the secrets of his home in hasty production. First he pointed to the bulletin board that hung above his kitchen table. There was a tattered black and white picture of him as a boy, standing among his friends. They were all emaciated. Their heads were shaved and they were dressed in prison rags.

"Not always this belly," Ernst said, again showing off his rounded stomach. "An American. He comes, takes photographs after Buchenwald liberation. You see?"

Bertram turned pale when Ernst rolled up his sleeve to show us the concentration camp number tattooed to his wrist.

"In camp I not eat, one month," Ernst said, waving a finger. "I survive. I never forget. Now food I always have. You hungry, you come to me."

This was his moment of triumph. A huge grin appeared across the old man's face as he showed off the contents of his cupboards and refrigerator. Cereal, pasta, rice, flour, sugar, every spice imaginable lined the pantry shelves. The freezer was packed with frozen steaks and fish. He kept apples and oranges, tomatoes and carrots in the crisper below. Cheeses, milk, yogurts, all kinds of deli meats and other juices crowded the middle compartments and a crate of eggs was in the corner.

"Do you have a big family?" I asked. I couldn't believe that he'd ever manage to eat so much alone.

Ernst looked confused. In the pause, he extracted his crust of bread from his shirt pocket and nibbled the edge. Then that crazed smile returned to his face. "I know what I cook you," he announced, taking a big frying pan off of the drying wrack. "I cook for you good German bacon."

Speaking a hopeless mix of languages, he explained the novelty of what he offered. "In Israel you can't buy so easy. Now I use Internet," he said, pointing across the room to an aging desktop computer, his method of importing forbidden meat. "Come to me," he repeated his offer. "I have bacon. I not keep Kosher. Nobody hungry."

Next we were treated to "good German bread." Ernst explained that he had baked the heavy black loaf several weeks earlier when his neighbor first alerted him to Bertram's presence on the kibbutz.

"But there is accident with tractor?" Ernst remembered. "I don't see you again so I put bread in freezer."

The old man was racing with energy. He used a big serrated knife to saw through the frozen bread and put a stack of slices in the toaster to thaw. Then he dropped a generous portion of greasy bacon on the already hot skillet, igniting steamy fumes and crackling oil.

Every condiment imaginable, jams, butter, cheese, hummus, honey, peppery spreads, sweet-and-sour dressings, appeared on the counter. By the time Ernst's table was set, the cooking smells had rendered us ravenous.

We sat down together. Ernst poured me another glass of schnapps.

"Come. You drink," he urged Bertram.

"I can't. I'm driving the tractor."

They argued in German, several back and forth negotiations before Bertram finally threw up his hands in defeat and took the drink that Ernst had poured.

"Prost," Ernst said, raising his glass. We both tapped him cheers.

The old man insisted on serving. Bertram and I didn't know what to say when he divided the entire portion of bacon, bread and greens between the two of us, leaving his plate empty. Neither one of us could begin eating without first settling the inequality.

"Won't you eat with us?" Bertram asked.

Ernst smiled oddly and again looked in his shirt pocket for that crust of bread. He held it up for us to see his teeth marks.

"All I need," he explained, taking a bite and pouring us each another round of schnapps. Again we said "prost" and drank at his command.

"Is no good? Eat. Eat!" Ernst encouraged us.

I ate, but Bertram looked sickly. His fork scraped against his plate. He was weak lifting bread to his mouth.

"Not feeling well?" Ernst asked.

Bertram answered in German.

When we left, the sun was already close to setting. Ernst continued to promise the fruit of his labors. "Come again. Eat. Never be hungry," he said, praising God of Israel for all his comforts.

"We will. I will," I answered.

Back on the hilltop Bertram was angry.

"What a bunch of robbers," he said, dwelling on his German past. "Nazi's even stole that man's stomach." Then he told me he'd made up his mind to leave the kibbutz. "You're wrong. There's no forgiving," he said. "Even if I laugh."

Ari's Mistake

This time Ari was on his own, driving west, crossing the country, camping nights. He drank coffee at the western diners he chose for breakfast and on the occasional bender, beer at lonely, tacky cowboy bars. Only two thousand miles into the adventure and already the daily act of filling the tank on the small, black VW Cabriolet was a reminder to him that he had come this far alone and that it was hard. When the car broke down, Ari blamed Myles, he blamed Melissa and he blamed his brother, Jeremy, for suggesting he drive west.

"Hello?" Jeremy answered his phone amidst horns, running motors and sirens.

"I'm stuck," Ari said.

"What?"

"I said I'm stuck."

"No. I can't hear. You're breaking—"

The call cut out. Ari let out a deep sigh, an irritable 'ahrgh!' filled with smoker's phlegm.

It was late afternoon. Warm yellow light peered through the heavy gray curtains in his room and when he peeled them further open, he could see the fence that hid the rumbling highway at the end of the parking lot, the little square pool and that hovering "Motel Six" sign. Ari grabbed another beer from the stash he was icing in the empty trashcan, searched all his pockets for the bronze key, found it on the night stand by the smoky, stained bed and swung the door open.

Squinting in the bright light, he dialed his brother again.

"That better?"

"A little. Where are you?"

"Nebraska. Omaha."

"How is it?"

"It isn't. There's nothing here."

"What's wrong with the car?"

"Everything. The catalytic converter is gunked up. I was on Route 90, trying to pass a truck. Couldn't accelerate past sixty. Barely made it to the dealership."

"And?"

"I'm going to kill you when I get home. You said you had her serviced."

"You mean the car?"

"Yes, the car."

"I did. But Jesus, Ar, you've done what, two thousand miles already? So you had a little car trouble. It's to be expected."

"Not a thousand dollars worth of car trouble. And that's not counting what I have to spend on this hotel while I wait for the part to get here."

"They didn't have the part?"

"No. It's in Michigan and it's the weekend. The part

won't come until Monday. Then they still have to service the engine. I won't be out of here till Tuesday."

"Are you in a hurry to get somewhere?"

"Not exactly. But it's four days and I'm stuck. Have you ever been to Omaha?"

"Ari, I'm driving. Can we talk later?"

"No. We can't talk later. This is your fault."

"Ari. Get yourself some beer. Maybe go for a walk? Does the hotel have a pool? At least it must be a nice sunset on the plains. I have to go. I'll call you later."

Ari paced and shouted into the phone, but his antics were a waste. His brother was far away in the East, laughing. Ari took a long, furious swig of his beer and hung up. Unable to swallow such a large gulp, he swished the beer in his mouth until he could feel the fizz climbing up his nose. Then he spit it out on the sidewalk. He was in a daze and he didn't realize that someone was watching.

"You need lime," the voice said, almost in the tone of a question. It was a quiet voice, colored by a soft, sunburned and patient Mexican accent.

"Excuse me?"

"Martín."

A tan man with weathered cheeks, thick black sideburns and a sweat-stained, San Jose Sharks hat pulled down over his eyes was sitting on the back of a red Ford pickup, stroking the ears of his fluffy mutt dog. He waved, but Ari was already trudging back to his room.

"You have more?" Martín called after him.

Ari was startled by the stranger's persistence. When he turned around, he saw the dog look up from his master's lap and tilt his head with nervous curiosity.

"More what?"

"Cerveza. You want? I teach you something."

The dog won him over. Martín let the mutt loose as he spoke his question and the dog bounded toward Ari, determined to sniff and slobber him affectionately. When Ari kneeled down to pet the animal, Martín got off the truck and walked stiffly toward Ari. He spun his arm around once to loosen up his shoulder. Dashes of white paint stained his jeans.

"Martín," the man said his name again, holding out a hand. Ari looked up.

"Ari. And this is?"

"El Perro? Sí. His name es 'Cali.' Is short for California."

"What kind is he?"

Martín began to laugh and he shrugged his shoulders.

Ari stood up. "Maybe some Australian Shepherd?" he said. "I like his pointed ears."

Martín smiled and scratched behind his neck. "Quizás," he said, still eyeing Ari's empty beer bottle.

"Alright. Wait here. I'll grab some more beers for us." Ari said, remembering Martín's offer. "I'm sorry, my Spanish is out of practice. Un momento?" He put a finger in the air to show how quickly he would return and then darted toward his room.

Ari was in and out, but Martín wasn't as fast. When Ari opened his door to the parking lot again, Martín was gone and Cali sat alone in front of his door with that curious quirked neck tilting his snout back and forth. Ari walked over to the dog, put the two ice-cold bottles down on the pavement and gave Cali a good rub behind the ears. Cali had soft, shedding fur. Ari admired the copper coloration around the dog's paws, stomach and tail and was pleased to learn that Cali knew English.

"Mano? Shake?" he asked, searching for the right commands.

When a door slammed at the end of the hotel block, Martín appeared carrying a green lime, packets of salt, a knife and a half-filled bottle of gold tinted tequila. He lit himself a cigarette as he limped along. Then he ushered Ari toward the back of his truck where Cali climbed up eagerly and was panting. Ari leaned his back against the cabin side and Martín dangled his heavy legs off the truck, same as before.

After handing over the beers, Ari lit himself a cigarette and watched Martín use the plastic-covered corner of the truck bed to chip off the tops. He handed one bottle back to Ari, told him to take a quick swig and then guzzled some himself.

"Not so much. Only poco," Martín cautioned, wiping his mouth and pointing to the level of his beer. Ari gave back his bottle.

The rest was a simple procedure. A slice of lime wedged in the neck of the bottle, a shot of tequila poured through, then a ring of sea salt spread across the opening. Martín prepared everything delicately. The sour drinks fizzed as he cleaned his knife with the bottom of his shirt and wiped the sticky limejuice off his hands onto his pants.

"Salud. To Omaha," he said, raising his bottle.

"To Omaha," Ari replied. "Now that's a name for a dog."

"You like?"

"I like."

The sun was sinking. The sky was smearing. Red. Orange. Pink. The whole color spectrum glimmered around the patches of clouds, but there was still an immense blue sky to paint. Cali started to lick Martín's open hand, his tail wagging as he enjoyed the tart salt caught in his master's fingernails.

"We should walk around," Ari suggested, pointing toward the hotel that obscured their view of the sunset. "You can't see anything here."

"No. I don't walk anymore today," Martín said. "Duele mi pierna."

"Your leg? At work?"

"Sí. Trabajo."

"Where do you work?"

There was a pause. Ari guessed that Martín was avoiding the subject of his visa status.

"Aquí y allí. I paint. I do maintenance."

"How did you end up out here?"

"Más trabajo aquí. Less work in California."

"You came here alone?"

"Mi esposa y mi hija viven en Mexico," Martín said, pointing in the direction he thought was south. "Mi daughter has sixteen years. All grown up."

Ari avoided the silence that followed by calling Cali.

"You like dogs," Martín observed.

"I do."

"Who do you talk to before on the phone?"

"That was my brother."

"He makes you mad?"

"My car broke down. I was angry. My brother was the one who convinced me to drive west. I was overreacting."

Their beers were going fast. Martín took the tequila bottle and offered to top Ari's off with another shot. Ari nodded and the lime sizzled as the sharp drink trickled through.

"Give it, you shake, como así," Martín said, showing Ari how to swirl the tequila into the beer. Ari thanked him and sipped cautiously. Now the drink was very strong and flat.

"I was sure you talk to woman," Martín said.

"You mean before?"

"Sí. When you were on the phone."

"No. That wasn't a woman. I don't call her anymore."

"¿Por qué?"

"Why? Because I can't. I mean, what the hell—"

"Lo siento. Never mind," Martín said, retreating.

"No. Please. You're fine. It's a simple story. I was engaged. My best friend, Myles, he slept with my fiancée. I had to get away so my brother lent me his car for the summer. Now I'm broken down. Bad luck adds up, you know? It's been a rough stretch."

"What was her name?"

"The girl?" Ari asked. He was considering lying and naming her after another city or state. "Melissa," he said, finishing his beer in one tough gulp. The force with which he put down his bottle startled Cali.

"Lo siento," Martín said again. Then he asked if Ari wanted to see a picture of his wife and child.

"Sure, quickly though, I have to make another call," Ari said, feeling buzzed and tired at the same time. He wanted to take a shower.

His joints lubricated by the alcohol, Martín was suddenly spritely. He hopped off the truck and eagerly went to the side door where he fumbled through the glove compartment in search of the picture. Then Ari felt the car battery click on. Martín rolled down the windows and put on some Latin music. When he came back around, he was smiling and looking at the picture of his family. He didn't climb back on board the truck. Instead he reached up and put the photo in front of Ari.

"Mira. Mi esposa, Inez, y nuestra hija, Raquel." The picture showed Martín, at least ten years younger and without his hat. Inez had dark hair and a plump figure. Their daughter was wearing a red flower dress, had dark black hair and a baby's smile. The picture was very faded.

"How long ago was this taken?" Ari asked.

"She is three," Martín said, pointing again at Raquel.

"How often do you see them?"

Martín shrugged his shoulders and started to return to the front seat to replace the photo in the glove compartment. When he came back he finished his story. "Mi esposa has new life now," he explained. "I want to come to California. She never want. Now I send money for Raquel and she live with other man. I forgive her."

Ari thought that was strange. He said that easily, "I forgive."

Sowly, Martín climbed back onto the truck and Ari offered him a hand.

"Gracias."

"De nada."

Cali came over and nuzzled his snout against Martín's neck.

"Do you call her?" Ari asked.

"Sí."

"And she will talk to you?"

"We still very close. Familia. Only it didn't work out."

"Don't you want to go back and see your daughter?"

"I leave, I lose everything here. My truck. Cali. No. I don't go back. No quiero. Too hard to cross again."

It got quiet after he said that. Quiet except for the steady traffic that kept rumbling across the highway and the salsa-fused Mexican music. Cali rested his head over the top of the truck, curious about the vibrations.

"Lo siento," Ari offered sympathy even though he didn't fully understand Martín's decision to stay in the States.

"Sorry for what?"

"About your family. I'm sorry you had to choose."

"I didn't," Martín insisted. "Una mujer siempre sabe lo que quiere."

"Lo siento?" Ari said, unable to translate.

"Woman always know what she want. Inez no me quería. She no like America."

Ari focused on the last flares of the setting sun. Martín took off his hat and combed his greasy hair. They sat together through the twilight hours, passing the tequila bottle, talking only a little and letting the drunk set in.

"If my friend were here, he'd keep us up," Ari said when he noticed his companion start to doze.

"Who?"

"Myles. My friend. He plays guitar. He loves a road trip. He's the asshole who—"

Martín stopped him. He remembered.

The sky was draining its colors and shadows were devouring the horizon. Ari's head began to ache. He stood up and yawned. "Guess it wasn't his fault," he said, stepping off the truck and stumbling on the landing. "If anything, it was my mistake."

"Cuidado." Martín said, peering down at his fallen companion. "No pensar demasiado en los errores."

Don't think on your errors. That was a drunk's advice. Martín offered Ari the last of the tequila, but Ari waved it away, a violent, acid burp creeping in his throat. He knew he needed to lie down or else he would be sick.

"Buenos noches y mucho gusto," Ari said, searching long and hard for that phrase in Spanish.

"De igual. The same," Martín replied.

"Hasta luego, Cali."

The dog lazily bowed his head before returning its gaze toward the dusky highway.

A short struggle with the key, then it was impossible to find the light in his hotel room. Ari tripped over the trashcan, spilling ice and water and soaking the knees of his pants. He tore them off and fell onto the bed. He was asleep, but his innards were busy. Gurgling tequila pains made him toss and turn. Whenever he opened his eyes, the room spun.

Hours later Ari heard his phone ring. He picked up without checking the caller ID.

"Ari?"

"Melissa? What time is it?"

"Where are you?"

"A hotel. Where are you?"

"I'm in New York. I haven't gone anywhere."

"The City?"

"Of course the City. Where else would I be?"

"I don't know. I miss you. I want to see you."

"Tonight?"

"No. Not tonight. When I get back to New York."

"You're not here?"

"No."

"Where are you?"

"Nebraska. Omaha. I'm stuck.""

"Nebraska? How did you end up out there?"

"Jeremy. Ask my brother. It was his idea. I was mad at you. I left."

There was a pause.

"Ari. Are you drunk? We shouldn't talk if you're drunk."

Ari wouldn't answer.

"Say something?" Melissa begged.

Ari asked her if she missed him.

"Of course I do. I miss you like crazy."

"Do you miss *him*?"

"Myles?"

"Yes."

"Ari, please. You're too drunk."

"Una mujer siempre sabe lo que quiere."

"What?"

"Do you miss him? I need to know."

Melissa was crying. "Yes. I miss him," she admitted. "I think you miss him too."

Ari climbed out of bed and turned on a light. His face in the bathroom mirror was yellow and bearded. A little water and his eyesight refreshed.

"Ari? Are you still there?"

Ari cleared his voice. There were a lot of questions coming into his thoughts all at once—questions he knew he had no right to ask.

"What do you miss about Myles?"

"I miss you, Ari. I miss you so much more," Melissa said, trying to stop his interrogation. But Ari had worked himself into the gutter and was determined to hurt her if he could.

"I don't believe you. You said you miss him. That means there's a lot still there."

"Ari, come back to New York. Let's talk then. Not like this."

"Tell me what you miss. Tell me everything," he demanded, kneeling on the floor to right the trashcan he had toppled and throw a towel over the puddle of melted ice.

Melissa answered carefully. "I miss you. I miss waking up with you and our walks in the city. I don't miss Myles like that at all."

"If you miss me so much then why did you do it? Tell me why it happened."

"We were getting married. Everything was happening so fast. I got scared, Ari."

"So you slept with Myles? Not good enough, Mel."

"What do you want me to say, that I didn't love you? You know that's not true. I messed up Ari. That's all that happened. I can't explain."

In a rush of blood to his face, Ari turned violent. He knew that if he yelled at her she would hang up.

"Yes, you can. Tell me what drove you away! What was *my* mistake?"

He yelled that into the phone several times, demanding an answer from the voice he no longer felt close to, but there was only static coming in reply. Slowly, he calmed down again. In his hand he held the curtain. Gently, he peeled the blinds open and witnessed the first glints of yellow light spread out over the parking lot. A sunrise. Morning. Welcome. Three days left to wait. He was glad to see Martín's red truck and Cali outside eating breakfast.

This Year in Jerusalem

Maybe I was homesick. When I heard Diné was back in Jerusalem after visiting her family in New York, I wasted no time.

"American Thanksgiving! We have to celebrate," I called up saying.

"Myles? Yes, yes, yes!" she said, loving the idea. We quickly made a list of things to cook and promised to invite all our friends. I took off work at the kibbutz that November Thursday and headed up to Jerusalem early. My plan was to visit my friend Tomer's bar and then play street music with a few Israeli musicians. After that, I'd help Diné cook.

On crowded Jaffa Street, I felt the usual shivers. Unnerved by those bearded black-capped men and the covered Arab women, I picked up my pace. Further down the road, taxi drivers were belligerent and stores were blasting

Holy Land music—tunes pulsing with pipes and strings and scratching Arab hymns.

When I was away from the crowds and chaos, I started to think things through. It was a confusing time for me. In many ways, I was opening a new chapter in Israel. Call it in the spirit of the holiday, for me it wasn't fall. It was the spring of my life. On the other hand, I'd often felt depressed and found myself shopping for flights. If I could face one friend from home, then I thought it might be a sign that I was ready to do the hard thing—go back to the States and apologize to Ari.

In the meantime, I was eager to meet my new friends. The evening promised the fulfillment of Tomer's bartending theory concerning the Holy City. "Jerusalem is a whole city tied and twisted up in knots," he had explained to me one day when were smoking hashish in the garlic field beyond the kibbutz. "Pull in one direction and you drag everyone else along."

I was interested to see how all the characters I had met in the course of several months of travel would mingle and I was glad that Diné had volunteered her home to host so many strangers. Above all, I was curious to learn what wildness Liam was up to. The last time we'd met, that lonely Brit dragged me off to Jordan on a binge to escape a fight with his fiancée. Now I wondered how he and Lilly were getting on with their peace work in Bethlehem. Had they patched things up?

Tomer's bar was down a vine-studded and limestone-floored alley. I ducked under the simple arch and through the red-ruby curtain that draped the entrance. Tomer was behind the rounded bar, pouring drinks for a girl. The space was small, yet wide and smelled of cinnamon incense.

My friend was happy to see me. Dreadlocks coiled over his shoulder, he lit a cigarette and introduced me to the girl at the bar. Her name was Nora. "Maybe you can help?" Tomer asked. "We're trying to think of a new name."

Nora lit a cigarette also and pointed to the floor. The old wooden sign, which said simply, in Hebrew, "Tomer's," was in the corner. I took a seat beside her and Tomer poured me a beer. Nora's stool wobbled as she turned and tucked a bare leg underneath the other. She had dark curling hair down to her chin and the greenest eyes.

"Tomer, yesh mashu shone? Ulai Jazz? You know I don't like this electric," Nora complained. As she dashed out her cigarette, little wrinkles appeared around her eyes, aging her slightly. Tomer laughed and went around to the back room where the CD player was hidden. Soon, a mysterious Klezmer-clarinet sounded, changing the atmosphere.

"What exactly would you say the theme is here?" I asked Tomer when he returned. I was still brainstorming names, trying to think of something very clever.

"Me, of course," he said. Then he pointed to the many self-defining talismans and souvenirs that were scattered about the bar. Cozy, emroidered pillows purchased from a Druze village up north lay on the floor. Tall Nargilas and a small bronze Buddha adorned the shelf above the bar. On the back wall, several framed, black and white pictures of different Old City and New City Jerusalem scenes were hanging. I smiled when I saw a picture of Tomer with his wife, Sarit, on a beach in India. Sarit's long, black-braided hair dangled over her tanned shoulders and Tomer wore his toothy grin. Unfortunately, Sarit had class that night and couldn't make the dinner.

"Did you take all these?" I asked about the pictures.

"Tomer is the best at photography," Nora answered for him. "I always show his work."

"You were at school together?" I asked.

Tomer shook his head. "Nora was my neighbor when we were growing—"

"Now I run a gallery," Nora interrupted.

Her English was direct and flirty. Her laugh was hoarse and tended to pick up speed. She was feeling very good, spinning in her chair and tapping her feet to the wild horn rhythms. When Nora suddenly surprised me with a hand on my shoulder, Tomer interrupted her dancing.

"Ha-che shniya," he said, pinching his thumb to his fingers in the Israeli sign to wait. As the song wound down, "I tricked you," Tomer announced, laughing. Lou Reed came on next.

There was a joke in Hebrew I missed.

Afterwards, "You're from New York?" Nora asked me. "I always want to go."

She spent the next several minutes explaining how she was trying to convince Tomer to come with her to America.

"It's what he needs. Don't you think?" she said, putting us both on the spot. "Manhattan will fix him. No more garlic farming on that kibbutz he's found down South. Artists belong in cities."

I was all too eager to please her. I gulped down beer and stated my general opinion that everyone in the world should see New York. Tomer, however, quietly dismissed the question.

"We'll go when Sarit is finished with school," he said.

Tomer had to run downstairs to change a keg. Meanwhile, I told Nora all about the day I had planned. I showed her the harmonica I had bought at the flea market in Jaffa and explained that I was waiting for a musician to call.

When I invited her to dinner, Nora was reluctant. "Ze too much. A hafta-ah. *Surprise.* I feel bad being hafta-ah."

"Come on. It's American Thanksgiving. Turkey Day!"

Food and promises of wine hardly tempted her, but when Tomer returned and explained that he was going also, she agreed to come. After that, Nora was all smiles. She insisted I visit her gallery before I meet the musicians.

"Come on, it's closed today. I give you private tour."

"You should go," Tomer encouraged.

There was no question. I finished my beer and stood up.

While I waited for Nora to use the bathroom, I asked Tomer what kind of girl she was. He poured me a chaser of Arak and told me we'd have a good time. Then she came back. At the door, Nora stood on tippy toes and Tomer bent down a little for her to kiss his scruffy cheek goodbye. Next she was holding my hand, leading me out.

"Lehitraot mame," Nora said, blowing kisses behind her.

"Rega! Wait," Tomer called. He was running after us, holding his sign.

"You're taller than she is," he said, sticking his tongue out at Nora and asking me to help pin the old sign back up. "I've decided to keep the name."

We were walking fast through a small neighborhood. Stray cats darted between the alleys and for a stretch it smelled like diapers. The gallery was housed in an old dome-topped building in the middle of a winding block. Nora pointed up at the window display where several brightly painted canvases were showing.

"Bo. Come," she said, rushing me inside. I watched her scurry around in her little loose skirt with the green and white print, turning lights on and arranging the mood. Suddenly she was gone. "Rega, don't look!" she called from a back room.

I looked a little. There was a lot of black and white

photography, schemes where light shone through streets. My favorite was one of a man's shadow meeting another shadow at the corner of the block.

"Lo tov. No good. You cheat," Nora said when she caught me peeking. Then she produced a bottle of cold white wine. She poured two glasses and we clinked cheers before beginning the tour. Tomer had two pictures hanging on the white walls. One was of Jerusalem in the snow. The other was of a sunset. Nora said his work had everything to do with time. "He speeds things up, he slows things down."

I watched her pull her hair back in a loose tie, leaving a strand shading her green eyes. Then she got an idea. "Wait here," she said, rushing out of the room again and bounding up the stairs.

I wondered about the flirting while I waited. I wondered why Nora insisted on so many "hafta-ah" surprises. They get witchy when they want something, I figured. At least it was that way with Melissa. I remembered how Ari's fiancée had suddenly started sitting closer to me whenever the three of us went out for drinks together in New York. I remembered Melissa calling more often and I remembered that time she put her hand on my leg. She was practically begging to cheat.

I sank back into the old drama. It couldn't be helped. Ari and I had grown up together. Unless I could get up the nerve to go home and apologize for sleeping with Melissa, a part of me was gone and tainted forever. No amount of wandering in the Holy Land would heal the wound.

"Hafta-ah, surprise!" Nora said when she reappeared. I laughed. She had dug out her own harmonica, a big one, with a slide for all the sharps and flats. Now she tucked her pinky between the slide and began breathing the wildest blend of fluttering notes.

"I start playing in the army," she explained after a few songs. She said it was the perfect instrument, small, and easy to learn, it helped her pass the time whenever she had to wait for a bus, or was on patrol. "I don't play for years," she admitted. Then I refilled her glass and we said cheers again.

The bottle was almost finished and the usual question; should I kiss her, should I not? was creeping up. I thought she obviously wanted something and that I didn't give a damn. If it was going to happen then it was going to happen.

It happened faster than I expected. Nora ushered me upstairs to her room. Bright light shone through the window across her white covered bed. Adjacent, there was a small couch and a coffee table with an ashtray and some glitzy magazines scattered on top. She kept an old Sony boom box in the corner. I watched her put on some soft Israeli guitar music and then sit down on the couch. Her legs were slightly open, and she patted the cushion where she wanted me to sit.

We made small talk, Nora impatiently explaining the small details of her decorating tastes and me commenting on the music. Finally I kissed her cheek. She smiled briefly, but didn't turn her head or reveal any emotions. She knew she had seduced me, but seemed to enjoy lingering on the point of decision where she still had complete control.

Next thing I knew she had pulled me close to her. My hand fell on her bare knee, and my tongue twisted in her mouth. I unbuttoned all her buttons and she unfastened my belt. When I followed her to bed she made me watch as she played with herself, gently swirling her swollen clit until the triangle of black hair above her slit glistened and I could hear the smack of her wetness.

Blinded by our haste, we both mustered false feelings, selfishly taking pleasure. First times are always a bit rotten like that anyway. Clumsy mistakes temper romantic hopes and motions. Then it gets lonely. There wasn't much noise. She bit my shoulder and left a mark. I hurt her when I went too fast. We both forgave each other and laughed when it was over.

When I noticed that I had missed the musician's call I didn't feel a bit like going. It was past three and I had told Diné I'd come at five. I sent a text and blew him off.

"Don't feel bad," Nora said, opening the window above the bed. "You waited all day for him to call."

I didn't feel anything. I kept my arm beneath her neck and breathed deeply. A cool breeze and chattering voices streamed inside. Nora had some American neighbors. They, too, were talking turkey.

"Yalah," I said, giving Nora another kiss. "It's American Thanksgiving!"

We got lost and then we found the place. Diné was stressed when she opened the door. Her summer freckles had faded from her cheeks and she was sweating. "You're late," she said, stretching her thin neck as her eyes darted toward the kitchen. She wore a flour spackled, blue apron and held a rolling pin at her side.

"It's my fault. I got us lost," Nora said. Then she presented the bottle of wine we had picked up along the way. For a moment, the two of them had a look on their faces like they had met before. They broke into a long dialogue in Hebrew, suggesting times and places until Diné finally guessed, "B-ha shuk. It was at the market! I was selling my jewelry." Satisfied, they hugged and kissed cheeks like old friends. Then Diné grew serious again.

"You better be ready to help," Diné said, ushering us both into the kitchen. I held out my hand and promised pumpkin pie.

Wonderful smells filled the narrow room. She had sweet potatoes boiling in a big pot. The turkey was in the oven, garnished in red and green spices and stuffed with rice and raisins. A sprig of celery jutted out from between the bird's drumstick legs and slices of onion boiled in the brown gravy that was drizzling out and quickly filling the foil-lined pan. All that was left to prepare were the pies. Diné had been cooking all day and I thought she would go mad when there came another knock at the door, interrupting her instructions.

"Goony! Bear! Zoar!" The three big men who entered, clumsily carrying their motorcycle helmets and wearing leather jackets, reminded me of the Three Stooges. Diné ran to greet them all with hugs and kisses and a mouthful of the Hebrew she so loved to speak. Modest introductions were made and then it was back to work.

Diné was getting nervous. "How many of your friends are coming?" she asked, but didn't give me a chance to answer. "You think there will be room? We need more chairs. Is your friend from the bar still bringing his puppy?"

"What puppy?"

"I saw Tomer yesterday and he said—oh never mind. Hurry!"

The next crises involved the apples and the pumpkin.

"There's no space left in the oven. No time to bake pies," she fretted.

"Diné, col beseder. The pies can bake while we eat the turkey. Why don't you take a break?"

She was reluctant, but when I told Nora to open a bottle of wine and fix Diné a drink, she relaxed. Then I started making piecrusts and I recruited Bear to wash the pile of dishes in the sink while the other stooges set the table and put on music.

Soon, Simon and Garfunkel sounded more like Thanksgiving than ever before and Diné and I were bumping shoulders, peeling apples, snacking on cherry tomatoes and talking memories. We both missed snow, sledding and snowball fights.

"Did you see Ari?" I asked about her trip to New York.

"It was such a short visit. I didn't have time," Diné answered, shifting uncomfortably. Then she drained her glass and remembered that she had to call her parents before she got drunk.

"Don't you want to call home?" she asked me on her way out to the balcony. I shook my head to her disappointment, and it was hard to hide my jealousy. My family hadn't celebrated the holiday together for years and the only friend I cared about had cut our ties. As I watched Diné pace back and forth on the balcony, smiling and laughing to all the sounds of home, I sought a distraction, anything to avoid thinking about the States.

Conveniently, the cooked pumpkin slices needed mashing. I found a deep bowl and got creative with the sweet spices, adding cinnamon, nutmeg and ginger. Meanwhile, I could hear Nora laughing and speaking fast Hebrew with the stooges in the other room. I tried to make out words I knew.

The sun was setting. Diné stayed on the phone a long time. Lonely, I escaped the kitchen and went to the bathroom. I tapped glasses with Nora on my way there, but refrained from kissing her in front of everyone. Still, we exchanged lustful stares and I felt sneaky having her sour smell and the soft latex slime of a condom stuck to me. I wanted more and I wondered if she would invite me back to her place that night.

When I came out, everything had changed. I knew right away that Liam and Lilly had arrived. The volume of voices was double, and Liam's too-big laughter echoed.

Liam looked like a newsy the way he leaned against the wall, sipped his beer and posed in his striped collared shirt, dandy pants and tilted cap. Never a stranger, he wasted no time moving about the apartment, jovially introducing himself to everyone while Lilly shied away. With warm, two-handed handshakes he was speaking fast, casually pointing out his fiancée and explaining our friendship. He had bumped into Diné in the doorway and for a second I thought I'd have to rescue her. His intensity was simply overwhelming.

"Oh Diné, Myles told me you'd be lovely. He's told me so much about you. You make jewelry, is it?" he asked.

Diné showed him her necklace and the rings on her fingers.

"How lovely," he said, staring so hard at the trinkets that Diné blushed.

Liam didn't stop there. He caught Lilly passing by and pulled her to his side. You see my Lil?" he declared, pointing to Lilly's pale white ears. "She needs a pair of earrings. Do you reckon you can manage something glittery?"

As soon as he had pawned Lilly off, he acknowledged me. "Now there's a chef," he said, making fun of the apron I'd borrowed from Diné. Then he asked me where a man could smoke a cigarette. I gave myself another pour of wine and showed him out to the balcony.

Outside, Liam's cigarette dangled from his chapped lips.

"Feckin thing. Bloody 'ell. Light!"

I told him I loved it when he cursed British. Then, puff, puff; he took quick drags and we said cheers.

"Did you bring the pictures from Eilat?" I asked.

"Got them here," he said, revealing his clunky camera and a cable. "Regrets. Had to delete a few."

"Have you and Lilly made up?"

"Aye. Suppose we have," he dodged, peering inside to see if Lilly and Diné were still talking.

"Don't feel so guilty," I said, trying to stop his face from changing. Already his shoulders were slumping at the thought of his infidelity and deception.

"I love Lilly, Myles. That's the truth."

"I know," I said. "You've explained everything. See how it goes. Maybe you ought to tell her?"

Liam shook his head. He didn't want to remember the breakdown he'd had on our binge. How he'd come back from a girl's hotel room crying and swearing that he'd never meant for his fling to go so far.

"Alright," I said, wanting to let it go. "Just between you and me then."

He was pleased, but he tensed up again when he heard the door slide open.

"Look what I found!" Nora squeaked. She was cradling a frisky white puppy with a curling tail and pointy ears. She kissed its fluff as she came out onto the balcony and the small dog squirmed in her arms.

"Whose is this?"

"Tomer's."

"He's here?" I asked.

"Just arrived. I can't believe he bought a puppy. Sarit is going to kill him," she said, letting the pup down and asking Liam for a cigarette. Soon the dog was prancing on soft paws, sniffing the air and pulling on my shoelaces.

Before dinner, there was a lot of talk. I talked to Lilly about the volunteer work she was doing in Bethlehem. She said she wished she knew more Arabic, but that the kids she was working with were "real angels." She was visibly frustrated with Liam. "I wish he enjoyed it more," she kept saying. "He's so restless. I don't think he enjoys it at all."

Tomer was drunk over the puppy. "She's never going to expect it," he told me repeatedly, imagining Sarit's reaction when he'd get home late and wake her up with the puppy's wet kisses.

Hebrew mixed with English, language mixed with wine until voices became indistinguishable in the chatter. Only Liam's loud laugh could pierce the other conversations. While I talked with Lilly, he told Tomer and Nora and two of the stooges about our trip to Jordan and Petra. From time to time, he looked to me to fill in small details of particular interest.

"Come on Myles," he'd say. "Tell about the jeep ride and our picnic in Wadi Rum. Tell about those gypsy carriages and the donkeys. Remember that drunk in Eilat?"

At last there was tapping on a glass. "Ha ochel muchan. Food is ready. Shev. Sit. Please." Big old Bear said, pointing to the golden brown turkey that stood at the center of the table, ready to carve.

Diné had taken off her apron and was standing outside the kitchen. She looked tired, but satisfied with her cooking. Beyond the turkey, the table was bursting with color; bright green salads, a bowl of buttered string beans and white almonds, the pot of orange, mashed potatoes, and a plate with candied carrots, purple beets and cranberry sauce. There were platters with hummus and tahini—a glistening puddle of spiced oil floating on top—and, of course, at Liam's direction, deep glasses filled to the brim with ruby-red wine.

There weren't enough seats, so the three stooges squeezed together on the couch and used pillows to boost themselves up. Diné asked me to carve the turkey while she made one last trip to the kitchen and put the pies in the oven. When she returned, I sat between her and Nora. Tomer's puppy curled up at my feet.

"Have you picked a name for him yet?" I asked across the table as the first dishes passed around. Tomer was about to answer when Nora interrupted.

"He's going to name it 'Tomer's.' Isn't that creative?" she said, sticking her tongue out at him.

Everyone's cheeks were rosy. Everyone was full of laughs. I sought Nora's hand again under the table. She played with it hesitantly, but kept watching Tomer in a way that displaced me. Embarrassed, I pulled away. Then Liam stood up and asked our host for an anecdote.

"I don't know the American tradition," he said, "In England 'tis only proper."

I watched Diné blush, but egged her on with the others. She had worked so hard. We were all very eager to hear what she had to say.

At first Diné stuttered, running a finger through her hair and nervously holding her glass in the air. Then she said "This year in Jerusalem" and joked about how long we'd been friends. "Ever since Hebrew school, when we were studying for B'nai Mitzvot; Myles never fails to make life interesting. He shows up in strange countries unexpected and invites all his friends over..."

The other guests laughed, but when Diné looked straight at me, swallowing a bit of her speech, I realized she knew more than she let on. She was worried I'd never go home and face the friend I'd betrayed, and this was her way of pushing me toward a decision. I didn't need to listen to the rest of her toast. Diné had me figured all wrong. I was already mouthing the phrase myself, "Next time in America."

New York-Tel Aviv-Baltimore
2009-2013

Jeffrey F. Barken, Cornell University
graduate and University of Baltimore MFA candidate
frequently reports on Israel news topics and Jewish
interest literature.

This Year in Jerusalem is based on his experiences living
on a kibbutz in Southern Israel, 2009-2010.

Author's Note

Curious travelers bound for Ireland will enjoy visiting Brushwood Studios, the family home and art gallery of Diana Muller, located in Sneem Ireland. Diana's brilliant ink drawings have helped bring the scenes of *This Year in Jerusalem* to life, and though we haven't had the opportunity to meet in person for many years, our collaboration on this project has been a remarkable and fulfilling experience. Countless Skype conversations, email chains and honest critiques have helped us inform and inspire each other's artistic ambitions. Additionally, collaboration on Monologging.org, a website I started as part of my degree requirement for the University of Baltimore, has enabled us to experiment with the infinite possibilities of multi-media.

Readers may be interested to learn the story behind our friendship. After spending a year studying at the National University of Ireland in Galway, in the spring of 2007, I decided to take two weeks to hike around the Ring of Kerry. Carrying a banjo and an awkward, vintage, metal frame backpack—stuffed with books, clothes, hard boiled eggs and jars of peanut butter and jelly for makeshift roadside snacks—I set out on a crisp April morning. No further than 14 miles into the trek, however, terrible blisters erupted on my feet, grounding me for two days at a hostel in the inlet town of Cahersiveen. Unwilling to make the same mistake again, once I was healed, I resolved to hitch rides the rest of the way.

Over the next few days, drivers dropped me from one town to the next and I was treated to a wonderful tour of the peninsula. I explored castle ruins, wandered gardens and played music on Kerry's crystalline beaches. I met countless characters including Joe Roddy, whose family operates the charter boat between Port McGee and the striking Skellig Islands. Roddy, an athlete and a stuntman in his youth, is a wonderful inventor and is famous for having been the first Irishman ever to stand foot on a surfboard.

Somewhere along the road, an artist named Jo-Anne Yelen picked me up. That day she was on a mission, sent by her brother Etienne to snap photos of his paddle across the bay in a homemade kayak. Here and there we stopped to climb cliffs, seeking a vantage point from where we could zoom the camera lens in on the black dot making strides across the water. As we drove, Jo-Anne told me about her family's unique art gallery in Sneem and invited me to spend the night when I made my way to their town.

Two days later I arrived at Brushwood Studios. I remember nervously knocking on their wooden door and asking for Jo-Anne. After all, it's not every day that families generously invite strangers to stay with them. Luckily, Jo-Anne's niece, Diana, who greeted me in the kitchen, soon put me at ease when she explained the Muller's long tradition of welcoming travelers to explore and share in the warmth and picturesque lifestyle their family has cultivated.

I was soon introduced to Diana's grandmother, Anne, and her parents Pam and Etienne Muller who encouraged me to stay as long as I liked. For the next four days I found myself immersed in their family's world of creativity and art. Blessed with a stretch of brilliant Irish spring weather, Diana and Etienne took me kayaking and I explored Etienne's woodshop. I enjoyed sipping tea on the patio with a beautiful view of the ocean behind me and Jo-Anne and Diana painting with the doors to their studios open. Later I played music with Diana's cousin, Andy. When she wasn't working, Diana and I talked about my ambitions to write, and spent the days exploring the woods and townships around the studio.

In my journal, I have it jotted down that I felt as though I had stumbled upon an artist's Utopia. A quick glance at the Brushwood Studios website today will demonstrate the breadth of collaborative arts in which Diana's family is engaged and the incredible talent each individual possesses. They are constant mentors to each other, sharing ample studio space where they can experiment and showcase the evolutions of their unique painting styles. When I finally said goodbye and Diana drove me to the bus station, I knew that we would keep in touch and that we would find a way to integrate our art forms.

Writers typically receive all kinds of advice about how to write the specifics of a scene. Prevailing theories advocate minimalism, a constant focus on only the essential facts that advance the plot. Regardless of what they've been taught, I think every writer fights a tendency to over-describe what their imagination is so powerfully projecting onto the page, and when they edit, wonder if they've cut too much, rendering the scene incomplete.

The opportunity to work with such a talented artist as Diana has provided me the rare chance to see my characters come to life through someone else's eyes. Although Diana has never traveled to Israel, I was immediately impressed by her ability to take details suggested in my stories and imagine what I had experienced during my year as a kibbutz volunteer.

In *This Year in Jerusalem*, Diana has used a homemade bamboo pen, black Indian ink and white acrylic ink to capture the shadows underneath a little boy's feet, the tensed pacing of Israeli soldiers manning guard towers, the many charged conversations between sparring characters, and the musical vibrations of a somber high. I am in debt to her for her tremendous commitment to this project and look forward to collaborating again in the future.

For more information about Diana and
Brushwood Studios, visit:

www.dianamuller.com
and
www.brushwoodstudios.com

Colophon

This book was designed by Jeffrey F. Barken. The text pages are set in Bell MT and Arbitrary. Stories are accompannied by Indian ink and acrylic illustrations by Diana Muller.

Made in the USA
San Bernardino, CA
25 April 2014